Hahn saw Taylor looking back at him and asked, "What is it, John?"

Taylor did not have time to  burning on his side and a mon echoing report of a rifle shot.

"Down," he shouted. "Get shooting at us." He bailed out of his saddle, hit the ground hard, and bounced to his feet waving his arms to chase his horse and pack animal back up the canyon where they would be safe.

Hahn dismounted too and had the presence of mind to grab his shotgun before Taylor ran back and spooked those horses to chase after the ones Taylor had already sent running.

Both men dropped behind the spread of dark juniper as another rifle shot rang out . . .

Other books by Frank Roderus

PAROLED
HARLAN
CHARLIE AND THE SIR
JASON EVERS: HIS OWN STORY

RANSOM

FRANK RODERUS

Dorchester
Publishing

DORCHESTER PUBLISHING

Published by

Dorchester Publishing Co., Inc.
200 Madison Avenue
New York, NY 10016

Trade book ISBN: 978-1-4285-1179-8
E-book ISBN: 978-1-4285-0994-8

First Dorchester Publishing, Co., Inc. edition: October 2011

The "DP" logo is the property of Dorchester Publishing Co., Inc.

Printed in the United States of America.

Visit us online at www.dorchesterpub.com.

RANSOM

Chapter 1

A small, nattily dressed man came around the corner onto Hardesty Street. John Taylor saw him and immediately shrank back into the doorway of Swofford's Farm and Ranch Supply. Taylor grimaced and hissed, "That son of a bitch." His knuckles turned white from the force of his grip on the handle of the hammer in his hand. "Bastard," he whispered. He felt an impulse to rush out into the street and use the hammer to smash Richard Hahn's head.

"Did you say something, John?"

"I . . . no, Mr. Swofford. I didn't say nothing."

"Oh well." The owner of the business hesitated, then gave Taylor a weak smile. "When you're done repairing that facing, John, I have some paint in here for it."

"Yes, sir. I'll only be a few minutes more on this. Figure I can put on the first coat soon as I'm done pounding nails an' the second coat this afternoon after lunch. How would that be, sir?"

A wagon rattled past, empty judging by the way the wheels bounced off the ruts they rolled over. The driver, Dean Caligan, raised a hand in greeting although whether to Taylor or to Swofford, John was not sure. Perhaps to both.

Taylor returned the gesture, Swofford did not.

"Fine, John. Fine," Swofford said, sounding like he did not particularly mean it. He turned and went back into his store. Taylor peered into the street. All he could see of

Hahn now was a glimpse of the SOB disappearing into the bank.

An image projected itself into Taylor's mind, an image so vivid and unsettling that his knees buckled and he reeled back against the door frame that he was working on. The image was of Jessie. Jessica Taylor, damn it. Taylor. Not Hahn. Never would be Hahn if he had anything to say about it. He visualized Jessie lying naked, the way he had seen and loved her so many times through the course of their marriage. In his mind's eye she lay open, loving, inviting. But the man she was inviting into herself was Richard goddamn Hahn.

Taylor squeezed his eyes tight shut against images he only imagined, but they remained. He could see them. Could hear Jessie's little whimpers and moans. The way she used to sound for him. For him, damn it, for him. He could imagine Hahn . . .

John's breathing quickened and his grip on the hammer tightened all the more. For one ugly moment his impulse to charge across the street and crush Hahn's miserable skull was almost overwhelming.

"John." Swofford had to repeat himself several times before he finally got Taylor's attention.

"Sir?"

"Are you all right, John? You're pale as a ghost. Are you sick?"

"No, sir." Angry. Sick to his furthest depths, he thought. But he said nothing.

"If you're not feeling well, John, you can finish this tomorrow. No harm done if you'd like to wait until then."

"No, sir, I . . . I'm fine. Really."

"If you say so. But if you change your mind, just let me know."

"Thank you, Mr. Swofford. I'm all right. Really I am."

"Very well. I'll be inside if you need me." He returned to his sales counter to be available if he was needed there.

Two of the town's respectable married ladies came by. They entered the store, their skirts swirling and trailing a delicate scent of powder. There was already one of the less respectable women shopping in there. That could lead to fireworks but probably would not. Each would ignore the other and very soon the soiled dove would fly out into the street and away to the edge of town where her kind stayed.

John crept a few feet forward, out toward the sidewalk, until he could see the front of the bank. There was no sign there of Hahn. No sign anywhere of Jessie. He felt, quite suddenly, like crying. But grown men of thirty-six with a wife and a child do not cry. Never mind where that wife and that child happened to be living at the moment. Never mind that the low-life son of a bitch Hahn was half John Taylor's size. Never mind the fact that John could break Hahn in half without raising a sweat and then break those pieces in half too. Lordy, he did want to do that. He would have too except for the fear of what Jessie might do if he maimed the bastard.

John regained control of his emotions, plucked a light finish nail out of the pocket of his canvas carpenter's apron, and went back to the job Mr. Swofford had hired him to do.

As expected, the lass of the evening came hustling out with her eyes brimming with unspilled tears and her cheeks red.

John whacked the finish nail. Hard.

* * *

Dick Hahn smiled and leaned across Randall Bonner's handsome desk. He accepted the papers the bank president handed him, fussily straightened them even though they were already straight, then slipped them into his folio and fastened the soft leather folio shut. "Thank you, Mr. Bonner. Seventeen hundred this quarter, hmm? The bank is doing well."

"We both are, Dick." The way the banker's waistcoat gapped between the buttons suggested that he was expanding quite as much as his bank's assets were.

"So we are," Hahn agreed. "You've held back a reserve for depositor payrolls and such?"

"Of course." The banker smiled. "Prudence, Dick. Prudence in all things. That is the way I see it. Always have."

"Sensible," Hahn agreed. Agreeing with his largest and most important client was all part of the business. "And your investments are liquid in any event. I shall get this 'buy' order away in tomorrow's mail pouch." He pursed his lips and nodded. "I really believe you will like this new security. I know the issuing agent personally. Met the gentleman when I was in Chicago last fall."

"What is the promised yield, Dick?"

"One and a half. I could get you another quarter of a point elsewhere, but for that I'd have to lock you in for a certain time. Better to keep things fluid in case of unanticipated need. I know you agree with that." He winked. "Prudence. Remember?"

Bonner laughed. "Yes, always."

"Are we all set for this quarter, then?" Hahn asked.

"Indeed. And don't worry, Dick. I'll follow with the transfer of assets as soon as I have the paperwork completed. A day, two at the most."

"Very well, sir, and I will have an updated report on the

bank's total portfolio in another few days. Just as soon as I have confirmation that these purchases have been completed."

"There's no rush, Dick. You know I have every confidence in you." Bonner reached for the humidor on his desk, offered a cigar to Hahn, who declined, and took out a fat, pale, very expensive Hernandez y Hernandez Presidente for himself. He used a silver cutter to trim the twist, then struck a match and lighted his smoke without bothering to first warm the tobacco. "Are you sure you wouldn't like one of these, Dick?"

"Thank you, but I don't smoke."

"Oh my," Bonner said with a shake of his head and a billow of exhaled cigar smoke. "You don't smoke. Don't run around with wild women either or I suspect I would have heard about it. Whatever do you do for fun?"

Hahn laughed. "Surely you don't expect me to answer that, sir."

"Surely I do not. Which reminds me, when are you and Jessie going to set a date?"

Hahn scowled. "When is that sorry son of a bitch John Taylor going to agree to the divorce? Jess has asked him for one. He continues to refuse her."

"I'm sorry, Dick. I didn't mean to bring up a painful topic. You know I'm pleased for you and Jessie. You make a wonderful couple and I know you will have happiness together."

"We do, sir. We already do." Hahn stood and tucked the folio under his arm. "If you will excuse me now, I need to get back to my office and prepare this order." He sighed. "You know, things will be so much easier once we get the telegraph extended this far."

"They say we should have a line in next year or thereabouts."

"It can't be soon enough for me." Hahn leaned forward and shook hands with Bonner. "Thank you for your business and for the trust you place in me."

"With every confidence. Really." Bonner smiled. "Will you be sitting in on the poker game tonight, Dick?"

"Now, Randy. You know my heart is pure."

"Never stopped you before, you old phony."

"Nine o'clock?"

"As always."

"I'll see you there." In truth, Dick Hahn hated the all but obligatory poker games Bonner hosted for a select few of his cronies. Those social events were important to his business, though. The participants were his primary source of clients. They were among the few in Thom's Valley who could afford to think in terms of investment capital.

Hahn turned and made his way out of the bank president's office and back to his own very nicely appointed small suite above Walker's Dry Goods.

When Dick Hahn first set himself up in business, those two rooms were bare planking and sharp splinters. He spent nearly everything he had to decorate and furnish his office. Appearances were paramount in the investment business and he wanted Hahn & Associates— not that there were any actual "associates" yet—to charm potential customers the moment they walked in the door. Polished wood, wool rugs, and warm colors gave an air of opulence that reassured everyone including Dick Hahn himself. And soon, he believed, his own personal fortunes would match the impression he displayed for the benefit of others. One or two more corporate accounts in line with Randall Bonner's and Dick Hahn would be well on the way toward genuine prosperity, perhaps even wealth.

Better yet, there was Jessie. There was always Jessie. In his mind and in his heart, there was Jessie.

Hahn was a happy man as he walked down Hardesty toward the comforts of his office.

* * *

"...seventy-five, eighty-five," Swofford mumbled, counting aloud as he slowly plucked coins out of his cashbox and placed them carefully on John Taylor's palm. "Ninety-five and a dollar. Exactly as agreed, right?"

"Yes, sir, and I thank you for the work. If there is anything else you need . . ."

"When there is you will hear from me, John. You do good work."

"Thank you, sir. Thank you very much." Taylor smiled and added, "Don't be shy about telling your friends." He dropped the day's pay into his pocket and backed away a pace or two, then turned and stepped out of the farm supply. He folded his apron, laid it over the long, shallow toolbox and carried it the four blocks to his shack on the edge of Thom's Valley.

He set the toolbox down on the kitchen table that took up most of the available floor space in the main room. Taylor yawned, stretched, and gave some thought to making himself supper.

That was a poor prospect. He had never been a good cook to begin with and had been away from the house all day long, so cooking a meal would involve starting a fresh fire and letting the stove top heat so he could put together a barely palatable meal. Bacon and beans were just about the extent of Taylor's abilities and neither particularly appealed to him this evening.

He thought about the fine suppers Jessie used to have

waiting for him. She was able to make this hovel seem a gracious home and the plainest of meals seem a feast.

But that was then.

John went out onto the porch to wash, then back inside for a clean shirt—the cleanest he could find anyway—and outside again.

He had money in his pocket and Joe Finnegan at Frenchie's Place served a fine free lunch. Or if a man wanted something more substantial than cheese, crackers, and pickles, Finnegan would provide a huge bowl of chili and a beer for fifteen cents. Chili sounded pretty good. Certainly more interesting than his own cooking would be.

John took a twenty-five-cent piece from his pocket and dropped it into the tobacco can on a shelf behind the stove. Rent money. He tried to have it ready when it came due. Usually did too. Jessie always had. She was meticulous when it came to money.

Jessie was good about other things as well. Life had been better when she was home. All of it. Lord, he did miss her. Missed the merry sounds of their daughter too.

He stuffed his shirttail into his britches, set his hat at a jaunty angle, and ventured out into the street ready for an evening of beer and billiards with the town bachelors. John had gotten away from all that back when he was married.

But then, damn it, he was still married, wasn't he? Not living together was not the same thing as not married.

She was still his. She always would be. He would never let her go. Never!

John pushed through the batwings at Frenchie's and surrounded himself with the bright, yeasty scent of beer and the masculine odors of tobacco smoke and sweat.

* * *

At the first of five chimes, Dick Hahn glanced at his wall-mounted Vienna Regulator clock, then at his pocket watch to verify that they had the same time. He pushed back from his desk and stood, buttoned the lower buttons on his suit coat, and stepped to the hat tree to retrieve his derby. By the time the fifth and final chime rang, Hahn was outside on the rickety landing—he really needed to have the steps on the side of Walker's Dry Goods reinforced—and on his way home.

Home was less than a quarter mile away, a modest bungalow with a covered porch across the front and a separate laundry in back. It was not the gracious, southern-style mansion he intended to build for Jessie someday, but it would do for the time being.

The scent of roasting meat filled his nostrils the moment he walked in the door. Little Louise, "Loozy," ran to take his hat. He handed it over and bent to claim a kiss from the child, then went into the kitchen and gave Jessica a considerably more impassioned greeting.

Jessie fluffed her hair, straightened her collar, and set a potholder aside. She looked, he thought, pretty as a picture. "How was your day, dear?"

"Fine. You know. Business." Dick removed his coat and hung it on the hat rack one arm below his bowler. He took a smoking jacket off a companion arm of the rack and put it on. Not that he smoked, but he liked the feel of the satin cuffs and collar, liked the idea too of being a gentleman taking leisure in his own warm domain.

"Was there nothing interesting?"

Dick thought for a moment, then shook his head. "No, not really. You?"

Jessie's eyes sparkled and her nose wrinkled with merriment. "As a matter of fact, dear, your wife has been invited to join the Trent Street Auxiliary." The ladies of the auxiliary were the cream of Thom's Valley's society. An invitation from them meant that Jessie and Dick were already overcoming their not-quite-yet marital status. The whole town knew about it. It delighted Dick that Jessie was not being penalized because of it.

"Well, well, well." He pulled her close and gave her a congratulatory kiss. And then another.

Jessie pushed herself away, her eyes cutting toward the parlor where Loozy was bent over a slate, copying letters in a flowing cursive script, penmanship being a highly regarded skill in Miss Semple's English classes. "Later," she whispered. She gave Dick a quick hug, glanced again to make sure Loozy was not paying attention to her elders, and gave Dick a much more intimate touch before she turned back to her oven. In a louder voice she said, "Dinner will be on the table in a moment. Why don't you get Loozy and the two of you wash up?"

Dick pumped water for Loozy and then she returned the favor for him, right there in the kitchen. An indoor pump was regarded as the height of modernity if not fashion, and Jessie proudly showed off her kitchen sink pump at every opportunity. Dick had had it installed just for her. He liked to indulge her.

Jessie had their supper on the table by the time Dick and Loozy were ready to sit down, roast beef and smoothly mashed potatoes and the usual trimmings. He knew it would taste as good as it smelled. Jessie was an excellent cook and kept an immaculate house.

The time would come, though, he thought, when they had servants to do the cooking and the serving and the washing-up afterward. But that time was not yet. Quite.

Dick Hahn was a very satisfied fellow when he picked up his napkin, shook it out, and tucked it into his shirt collar.

* * *

John felt a light touch on his elbow. Beer in hand, he turned to see a middle-aged man with a graying beard and bright, lively eyes. "Hello, Anse. Buy you a beer?"

"Thanks, but you know good and well I don't drink."

Taylor laughed. "Of course I do. Why else do you think I felt safe to offer."

"One of these days I just might take you up on such an offer," Anse Edwards warned. "But not now." He became serious for a moment. "I haven't had a beer in eleven years."

John nodded and set his own beer on the bar. He had not known Anse in those days, but he understood that the friendly rancher had been something of a rake in his younger days. He stopped drinking and hell-raising when his boy was born and had not taken a drink since. "If you won't let me buy you one, what can I do for you, Anse?"

"I came in looking for you, John."

"For me? Uh-oh. Is something wrong?" He retrieved his mug and took a swallow of the crisp, heady beer.

"No, not at all," Edwards said. "I was wondering if you'll be free to do some work at my place in a couple days. It's only for one day's work, though."

"Two days from now? Sure. What is it you need, Anse?"

"I need a mugger to help me brand some cows. I bought forty head from Wallace Brandell. They'll be delivered tomorrow. Wallace and his boys will drive them over.

I don't want them standing in my pen too long. Better if they get out to find their own grass, but I want them branded before I turn them out.

"Bobby can work the gate and keep the irons hot for me, but I can't very well rope them out of the pen and throw them too. Big as you are, John, you're probably the best man in this whole valley when it comes to mugging cattle. Can you do it?"

"Sure. When do you want me there?"

"Well, you see, that's another thing. This might go slow, so I'd like to get at it as early as possible. I was thinking maybe you could come out to the place, like, tomorrow night. Beatrice will give you your supper and I'll pay you extra for the time. That way we can get started at can-see and work on through 'til the job is done. Or until it's complete can't-see if we really have trouble with them."

"Are these some of Wallace's range cows?"

Edwards nodded. "They are. Mostly fours and fives. Still with good breeding years ahead of them, but they sure as hell aren't anybody's tame barnyard cattle. Even you, big as you are, might could have trouble getting them off their feet."

John Taylor, six feet three and powerfully built, said, "Big has nothing to do with it, Anse. It's all in the leverage, that and knowing how to do it. But all right. I know how to knock a cow down. I can hold 'em while you and the boy do the branding." He chuckled. "Besides, I've et your lady's cooking before. I'd be proud to sit at her table any time. Tell you what. I have a couple hours of work to do for Will Renfro tomorrow. I'll get that done in the morning and ride out to your place in the afternoon. In case you might need help penning them. Anyway, I'll be needing a way to get out there. I'll have to ask you to pay for the rent of a horse."

"You go ahead and get one. I'll reimburse you for the cost."

John grunted. "Two days like that, it'll cost a dollar."

"That's all right. A dollar for the horse and, say, two for your time. Would that be all right?"

"You have yourself a hired man, Anse."

"Fine. Tomorrow evening, then."

"I'll be there." John grinned. "Sure I can't buy that beer for you, Anse?"

"If I was to come home drunk this evening, Beatrice would have my ears pinned to the gatepost before dawn."

"Mind if I have another?"

"Let me buy you one," Edwards offered.

John grinned down at the smaller man. "That, sir, is an offer you won't hear me refuse." He reached for the beer already in hand and tossed it down, then rapped the mug on the counter to call for a refill.

* * *

"Someone is at the door, dear. Can you get it? I'm in the middle of something."

Dick Hahn stood and took a moment to button his suit coat before stepping out into the parlor and then to the front door. He had heard the rap on the door as well as Jessie did but waited for her to respond in the hope that he would not have to get up.

Hahn pulled the door open and smiled. "Good evening, Anselma. Come in."

"Is the little one ready, senor?"

"Yes, of course, but you will stay here with her, won't you?"

"Mrs. Hahn said it will be all right if I take her with me

to my place. She can play with my children. But do not worry. I will watch over her with care, senor. She will be good . . . I mean . . . fine; she will be fine."

"Mrs. Hahn said that, Anselma?"

"Sí, senor, she said." Anselma bobbed her head nervously. Probably afraid he was going to refuse her the job of watching Loozy for the evening, he thought.

"If Jessie said it, then I suppose it's all right." Dick stepped back from the doorway.

The Mexican woman came inside, her posture diffident.

"Wait here. I'll get Loozy." Instead of Louise responding to the babysitter, though, it was Jessica who appeared in the parlor first. Dick went back into the kitchen to sneak a sip of Kentucky corn nerve tonic before they had to leave. Randall Bonner's dinner parties were always bone-dry thanks to Bonner's wife, Abigail, and the contract bridge the Bonners played at their soirees were just as dry. Confusing too, as the rules were too close to whist. Dick constantly got the two mixed up, which led to disastrous play. That was a mistake Jessie never made. But then she cared about the play while Dick did not. The Hahns had to stay in the Bonners' good graces, though, if Dick expected to get ahead. As for Jessie, she was delighted simply to be in the same social company as the bank president and his wife.

Jessie finished giving Anselma her list of instructions, then went to fetch Loozy, who would have been more than content to simply stay in her room by herself with a book or a doll for company.

The child came scampering into the kitchen, rose on tiptoe, and gave Dick a rather wet kiss on the cheek. "Good night, Dick."

"Good night, sweetie."

"Have fun," she said.

"You too."

Loozy's response was a sigh and a sour face. But she went dutifully off to be collected for her version of an evening out. She did not like playing with Anselma's children, as they did not speak English and she had no Spanish.

Dick marched into the parlor behind her, arriving in time to see the front door pulled shut and Jessica facing it.

"Lovely," he announced.

"Do you like it?" she asked, turning and holding the skirts of her gown out for display. The gown was a medium blue with white trim and a neckline that was just short of being revealing.

"Love it." He meant that. It looked good on her. Virtually anything looked good on Jessica, though. "Is it new?"

She nodded. "I picked it up this afternoon. Had it made especially for this party. Do you mind?" She twirled around so he could enjoy the view from all sides.

"Do I ever mind indulging you?" He wrapped Jessica into his arms and held her close, her breath warm and pleasant on the side of his neck. "Hmm," he said, "do you think we'd be too, too late if we, um . . ."

She pulled away and gave him a playful slap on the chest. "Mind your manners, mister. We promised to be there."

"But did we promise to be on time?" Dick countered.

Jessica ignored him. She turned and went into the bedroom to finish dressing.

Ervin Ederle

Erv "Big Man" Ederle raised his mug and thirstily downed the golden brew it contained. "Good. Damn good." He slammed the empty pewter mug down on the rough-hewn bar and growled, "Another."

The barman looked at him with unconcealed skepticism and said, "When I see your money." Erv had imbibed there before, it seemed. And he was a very difficult man to evict.

The man flinched when Ederle's hand jerked down and back, but it was his pocket he dug into and not his holster. He came out with a small pouch, opened it, and extracted a ten-dollar gold eagle. "There, damn you. Now will you pour the damned beer? And add a shot to go with it. Hell, add a bottle, and keep the beer coming."

"Yes, sir." The barman was visibly shaken. Ervin Ederle had some years on him—half a century's worth if the truth be known—and his hair was graying, but he still had the demeanor of a man who was not to be trifled with, and he had enough guns and knives hanging about his person to bolster that impression.

Ederle drank until he was knee-walking drunk, tossing back rye whiskey one after another and chasing each swallow with a full beer mug, then found a corner where the sawdust was soft and welcoming and went to sleep there, his snoring rattling the rafters with each snort and flutter. In the morning he woke quite unconcerned about his choice of resting place, stood and brushed himself off, then staggered to the bar.

"Gimme an eye-opener," he roared, pounding his fist down and eyeing the bartender, one he had not seen the night before.

"All right. Beer or a shot?" The gent continued polishing glasses with a towel that was in bad need of washing.

"Both. An' be quick about it," Ederle roared.

"Fifteen cents," the barman told him.

"I got change coming from las' night. Now hurry up. My head is splitting an' I need a drink."

"Change? The hell you say. Now pay up or take off." The bartender reached under his counter.

Ederle mumbled some highly uncomplimentary claims about the bartender's habits and ancestry, but he reached for his pocket once again.

This time he came up empty. "I been robbed, you son of a bitch. Some bastard stole my poke. Where the hell is it?"

"If you don't have any money, then you'd best get out of here." The bartender's hand under the bar surface emerged, this time holding a cudgel. "Right now would be a good time for you to do that, mister."

"But damn it . . ."

"Now. I won't tell you again." He was not intimidated by the big, bleary-eyed drunk in front of him. He waved his cudgel menacingly and cut his eyes toward the door.

Ederle, unshaven and with his hair in wild disarray, picked up his hat and jammed it onto his head. He wobbled a little, then righted himself and headed for the batwings. He stepped out into bright daylight, broke and miserable and without even the price of a beer in his pockets. The sunshine stabbed his eyes, the pain causing him to squint, closing first one eye and then the other while he tried to navigate across the street.

The only good thing about the day was that his stomach was so sour that the mere thought of food made him want to puke. Some more. The stink on him suggested he had already puked all over himself sometime during the night. The good thing about that was that he had no desire for the meal he could not afford to buy.

But he had his guns. And he had a horse. Somewhere. He would just ride out until he came across a traveler. Someone alone if possible or at least not too many of them at once. And he would rob the unfortunate son of a bitch.

He belched, gave serious thought to puking again, and stumbled down the street toward the livery, hoping like hell he had had the foresight to pay for the horse's board in advance.

* * *

"Whoa. You dumb sumbish." Erv reined to a halt, then turned crossways to the road and looked up and down in both directions. He could not see anyone. Which was a shame because his stomach was beginning to settle. That meant he would be hungry soon. He knew himself well enough to anticipate that. What he needed now was a traveler.

But then for a man in Erv's line of work, patience was more than a virtue, it was a necessity.

The sun was a good half hour higher when he saw a dark speck approaching from the east. Two specks. Erv smiled. As the specks grew into recognizable forms, they appeared to be a Mexican peasant wearing white pajamas and a straw sombrero leading a donkey loaded with pale sticks. Firewood, he supposed.

It was a pity the Mex was not carrying something useful, but what was a man to do?

Erv rubbed his chin and hooked a knee around his saddle horn. He did not mind waiting now that he had the fellow in sight.

* * *

Ederle sat cross-legged in the shade of a cottonwood while his horse cropped grass nearby. He had his hat upended in his lap. The sweat-rimed hat held the take given up by that Mex peon who had had the misfortune to be on the same road at the same time as Ervin "Big Man" Ederle.

Big Man my ass, Ederle told himself when he was done counting the nickels and pennies he had taken from the Mexican. Old Man was more like it now. Dumb Man. Robbing for nickels and dimes. There had been a day when a dozen men felt privileged to ride with the Big Man. They took down big money. Banks, stagecoaches, once even a train. They had all fallen to the Ederle Gang.

Then Erv's luck began to turn bad. Too much shooting for too little return. Gang members died or were crippled. Replacements were slow to come. The size of the gang dwindled until the final small core of three men pulled out and went their own way with Johnny Baggs taking the leadership that rightfully belonged to Erv.

Thousands of dollars had passed through the hands of the Ederle Gang back in the old days.

Now he had . . . three dollars and fourteen cents.

He stood, his knees aching and his hands hurting the way they had begun to do of late.

He was getting old, damn it. That was the truth of the matter. He was getting old and tired and he wanted to find someplace where he could settle down and stay. Someplace warm. Someplace where there would not be posters out on him or posses to worry about.

Mexico was the most likely spot or down toward the border in Arizona Territory. It was kind of nice down there. Or had been the last he was there, which was quite a while back now. Before the war back East? He thought so.

He could find a little shack not too awful far from a store. Take in a little brown-skinned woman to do for him. Erv was partial to the dusky ladies. She could cook his meals and wash his clothes and, well, whatever else. He might be old but he was not that old yet.

That was what he needed. It would take money to do it, though. A helluva lot more than three dollars and fourteen cents.

What he needed, Erv Ederle thought, was one big—really big—score for his last take.

What he needed, he realized, was a plan.

Two days of close observation later, he had one. A really good one, he thought. And with a bit of luck he would not even need a gang to pull it off.

Chapter 2

John Taylor reined to a stop in front of the shack he still kept in the hope that he would bring Jessie and Loozy back into it where they belonged. He sat on the Slash 3 7 horse for a moment before dismounting. Turning to the youngster beside him, he said, "Care to come in for a snort? I have a piece of a bottle laid by for emergencies like this."

The boy, who went by the moniker Dink, shook his head. "Thanks but I got t' get these horses back to the ranch." He smiled and added, "Before Coosie bars the door an' quits serving up grub."

"All right. Suit yerself." Taylor swung his huge frame off the animal and quickly stripped the horse of his saddle and bridle. He clipped a lead rope to the halter and handed the end to Dink. "Listen here for a minute."

"Yes, sir?"

"I was watching you today. You're good with them cow critters. You'll be drawing top-hand pay here direc'ly. Count on it." He dropped his saddle onto the stoop in front of the door and rubbed his left shoulder where a cow had hit him a glancing blow with an unexpected kick earlier in the day.

"D'you mean that, Mr. Taylor?" The boy looked pleased.

"It's John, boy. Nobody named me Mister. An' yes. I do mean it. You got the makings of a right fine hand." He smiled and extended his hand to shake.

"Thank you, Mi . . . I mean, John. Thanks a lot." He grinned and tightened up on his reins to back his horse away a few paces, Taylor's borrowed mount following.

"Get on back now before you miss out on your supper."

Dink touched the brim of his floppy old hat in farewell and reined his horse back toward the Slash 3 7, dragging along with him the animal Taylor had ridden into town.

Taylor shouldered his tack and carried it inside. Jessie always insisted that he keep his saddle on the porch, but John worried that would allow mice to get after the leather. Now that she was gone he kept it inside where it belonged.

He stared at the long cold stove and considered what he might cook. If he still had anything in the place that was fit to eat. He had been gone eight days working for Tweed out at the Slash 3 7 and had no idea what he had in the place to eat at this point.

Which was all the excuse he needed.

Taylor pumped some cold water into the copper sink and made quick work of washing away the dust he had collected on the ride in with Dink. He changed to a reasonably clean shirt, battered the road dust off his britches, and headed for Frenchie's Place.

"H'lo, John," Finnegan greeted him. "Beer?"

"Damn right. I'm parched." He hooked a boot onto the brass rail that ran along the floor in front of the bar and planted his elbows on the countertop.

"Where've you been, John?" Finnegan asked as he reached for a mug and shoved it under a spigot.

"Working." He grinned. "So's I can pay your outrageous prices."

"Good. Be all right with me if you just hand over

whatever you got paid." Finnegan winked. "Or I can take it a bit at a time. You want some chili with that beer?"

"That's the best offer I've had in a while."

Finnegan stuck his head through the door into the back of the place and yelled, "That big ape is here and he's wanting some of your best chili."

John heard some laughter from the kitchen. Finnegan came back and drew the beer, blew most of the head off, and filled the heavy glass mug the rest of the way to the brim. "Drewry's been looking for you," he said as he slid the mug in front of Taylor.

"Drewry. What the hell does he want with me?" Leonard Drewry worked for the court over in the county seat. The man rarely put in an appearance in Thom's Valley, and whenever he did it was usually for some unpleasant reason.

Finnegan shrugged and said, "I haven't heard, John. Is there, uh, is there any reason why you might want to stay out of sight?"

"Nothing that I can think of, Joe." He pondered the question for a moment, then shook his head. "Nope. Nothing."

"Then just stick around. Drewry's sure to find you."

"I got no reason to hide from him. No reason to go running to find him neither." He belched and said, "Damn but that beer tastes fine. Draw me another, will you?" He laid a silver dollar on the bar to assure Finnegan that he had the wherewithal to pay for his evening, then reached for the bowl of roasted peanuts a few feet down the bar.

* * *

"Pull!" The boy in the pit gave the clay ball a heave. The target curved into sight at an upward angle and flew high. Dick Hahn's handsomely crafted English double lined up on the flight of the ball, swept slightly ahead to compensate for the time it would take for the load of light shot to reach the target, and with a touch of Hahn's finger spat shot, flame, and smoke into the clear air.

Ten or so yards to the fore, the clay ball burst into a puff of dust as Hahn's pellets struck it dead center.

"Nice, Dick. Very nice."

"Thanks, Willis." Hahn swiveled the release lever to break the action. He plucked the spent shell casing from the breech and tossed it into the bucket beside his shooting station. At the end of the day, some club employee would gather the empties and take them into the equipment shed to reload. Dick assumed that was where they also molded the clay targets ready for the next weekend of shooting, but he had never been interested enough to ask. He was above that sort of thing now. Above that sort of person.

His companion stepped up to the board that marked the shooting position, shouldered his engraved and gold-inlaid German over-and-under, and cried, "Pull." Another clay flew high. Willis's gun spat, but the clay sailed on unharmed. Willis Hammerschmidt fired again with no better result.

"Next time, Willis. I thought you were on the bird this time."

"Right. Next time. Say, thinking about birds, did you hear there will be a live pigeon shoot over in Cauley next month?"

"No, sir, I hadn't."

Willis scratched himself and reloaded his gun, then said, "Chic Fullbright rounded up practically his entire barn full of passengers the last time the migration came back north. He's been feeding them cracked corn all this time." Willis laughed. "And catching hell from his wife the whole time too. Anyway, he is donating them all. Ten dollars a gun. All the proceeds go to Mrs. Dollman's orphanage. They get the dead birds too to bake for the kiddies."

Hahn nodded. "Sounds fine, Willis."

"Can we count on you, Dick? You're Thom's Valley's best wing shot and you know we want to make a good showing against those boys over in Cauley."

"Of course I'll be there." Hahn dropped a pair of fresh shells into the open barrels of his gun but left the breech open.

The two of them stepped over to the next station and Dick motioned for Willis to take the first shot.

Hammerschmidt snapped the breech of his shotgun closed, put the gun to his shoulder, and yelled, "Pull" again. The gun spat and the clay bird flew on to shatter when it hit the ground.

Hahn was feeling in a mood to show off a little. He closed the action of his shotgun and held it at waist level, then called, "Give me a double this time."

"Yes, sir."

"Pull."

His gun roared twice and powdered both birds.

* * *

Taylor scooped up another heaping spoonful of Maria Theresa Valdez Finnegan's chili, wiped the resulting sweat off his forehead, and grinned at the lady's husband. "Singe the hair right off a man's chest, that will," he said.

"Too hot for you, John?"

"Hell no. You know better'n that. Can't get too hot for this ol' boy." He picked up another heaping spoonful and shoveled it into his mouth. Good heavens but Joe's wife did make fine chili.

"I have some habanero squeezings here if you'd like some. It's been known to make strong men weep and turn boys into men, but if you'd like some . . ."

"Maybe next time," Taylor said with a laugh. He had tried Maria Theresa's habanero pepper juice once before. And only once. There would not be a second time. John Taylor was brave but he was not stupid.

"Another beer, John?"

"Reckon I wouldn't say no to such a thing as that."

Finnegan took John's half-full mug, refilled it from the tap, and returned it without touching the change that lay on the bar. "Crackers?" He shoved the free lunch tray closer to Taylor.

"Sure." John took a handful of the crisp soda crackers, crumbled them up, and dropped them into his chili. Lordy, but Maria Finnegan did know how to make a fine chili. If it weren't for her cooking, Taylor likely would have starved to death shortly after Jessie moved out.

"Something wrong, John?" Finnegan stopped what he was doing and stood looking at his friend.

"No." Taylor shook his head. "No, of course not."

"I thought . . . Never mind." Finnegan went back to polishing the clean mugs.

The batwings opened with a creak of rusty springs. Everyone in the place—there were a baker's dozen patrons there at the moment plus Joe and, in the kitchen, Maria—turned to see who came in. Everyone other than Taylor made note of the arrival and went back to their own conversations. Taylor scowled.

"Don't think you can sneak out, John Taylor. I see you there. Don't think that I do not."

"I ain't going no place, Drewry. What d'you want?"

Leonard Drewry marched across the sawdust to square off in front of John. He took a folded paper from inside his coat, cleared his throat, and handed the document to John. "This is official service of an action filed against you by Richard Acton Hahn. You are ordered to appear before the Honorable Curtis Cooper on the twenty-third day of June next."

"What's it about, Leonard?"

Drewry's upper lip curled. "Read it yourself. If you can."

John grunted. "All right, asshole. What day o' the week is that?"

"It is a Monday."

"Fine. You delivered your paper an' got to feel like a real grown-up man. Now get the hell outta my sight. You're ruining my appetite."

Drewry started to turn, but John stopped him. "Wait a minute, Leonard. There's something I'd like to ask you."

The process server turned back to face Taylor.

"My question is, does your mother know you're such a shit, Leonard?"

Drewry bristled but he was a head shorter than Taylor. The man had legal authority and he was armed while Taylor was not. Even so he did not want to start something or he would find himself out in the middle of the street wallowing in the road apples there. Instead he turned and rather stiffly marched back out into the night.

* * *

Hahn unfastened the bottom two buttons on his waistcoat and sat in his favorite chair. Loozy ran to get his slippers— it was one of her regular chores and it seemed to please her that she was given responsibility in the household—

while Jessica fetched the footstool and the lamp stand. Dick picked up the mail he had collected from Thom's Valley's tiny post office after the afternoon coach unloaded. He laid the latest *Rocky Mountain News* in his lap to be perused after everything else was digested, then took out his penknife and meticulously slit each envelope open.

There were three, two from his brother back in Illinois and one from Jessica's mother in Denver. He opened Jessica's mail but did not read it before passing it to her.

"Is there anything new from Danny?" Jessie asked when Dick set his mail aside and picked up the newspaper.

"No, not really," Dick said from behind the wide-spread newspaper. "He's thinking of standing for office next term."

"What office, dear?"

"State house. Could I trouble you for a drink, dear? Brandy, please. Neat."

"State house?" Loozy put in. "Isn't that like the jail? Why would he want to go there?"

Hahn laughed. "No, sweetie. I mean the state house of representatives."

"Would that make him famous?"

"No."

"Important?"

"Just so-so."

"Oh." Loozy went back to her schoolwork, her interest diminished if it meant this "uncle" she had never seen would be neither famous nor important. After a few moments she looked up again. "How is some brandy neat and some . . . um, what would that be? Sloppy?"

"Neat means without water, dear," Jessie put in.

"Oh." The child made a face.

"Have you tasted Dick's brandy? Is that what that face was all about?"

Loozy pretended not to hear and Jessica did not pursue the question. But it was obvious that Loozy had tasted some sort of hard alcohol.

"Dear," Hahn said.

Jessica looked up from her knitting.

"If things keep on the way they are going, I think we might be able to hire house help full-time. Someone to help you cook and do the heavy work. Would you like that?"

"Of course. Could we have Anselma come in full-time? She wouldn't need to sleep in." Jessica did not state the obvious, that their house was really too small to have live-in help.

"Anyone you like," Hahn said.

"When will we know?"

"If next quarter's numbers stay as high as I expect, we can go ahead, I think." He raised his newspaper, then lowered it again. "I saw Leonard Drewry in town this afternoon. I think he served John."

"Daddy?" Loozy said, sitting upright.

"A business friend of Papa's," Jessica quickly said. She gave Dick a cautionary look that said this was something they should discuss at another time, when John's beloved daughter was not listening.

Jessie knew about the suit, of course. Dick would never have filed it without her knowledge. Jessica was not entirely sure she agreed with it, but she was aware.

Jessica laid her knitting aside, gathered her skirts, and stood. "Is anyone in this house interested in a cup of cocoa?" Loozy's "yes" and Dick's blended into a single sound.

Ervin Ederle

Big Man Ederle sat on the rickety chair, his perch made all the more precarious because of the presence of the chubby woman on his lap. Erv brushed the spill of jet-black hair back from her ear and nuzzled the side of her neck. That prompted a fit of giggles and squirming.

Erv laughed and shoved his hand down the front of her blouse.

"No, no. The childs. Not in front of the childs."

If they were to do anything at all, it pretty much had to be in front of the children. The shack had only one room and it was none too large. There was no bed, just the table, two chairs, and an assortment of stools.

"Then get rid of them. I'm wanting some of what you got to give here."

"Wait." She stood and clapped her hands to get the children's attention—there were four of them at the table playing with the remnants of their suppers—then said, "Out. Out now. I will talk with Mr. Man in the, ah, alone, por favor."

The children, who seemed to range in age from roughly three up to perhaps nine or ten, frowned but they did not disobey. They left what they were doing and trudged outside.

Their mother shooed them along, then unhooked the tattered blanket that served as a door and let it fall over the opening. She went to a corner and produced a rolled pallet of woven cactus fiber. Bending, she spread that on the floor, then unceremoniously stripped off her blouse and dropped her skirt to the dirt floor. She was not wearing any undergarments.

She was flabby and not especially attractive. But she was female and she was there.

Erv Ederle chuckled, then stood and began unfastening the buttons at his fly.

"Hurry please, Mr. Man." She lay down on the pallet and arranged herself for his convenience.

"Hell, woman, I'm in no hurry. No hurry a'tall." Erv grunted as he got down to floor level.

"I must go soon, Mr. Man. I have work tonight." She reached for him.

"Work! What the hell kinda work do you figure to do at this hour? You ain't whoring, are you?" He seemed oblivious to the fact that she was selling herself to him in exchange for a smile and a handful of beads he had stolen from the mercantile that afternoon.

"Oh no, Mr. Man. I have to watch over the daughter of a rich man. He pays very good." She laughed. "He thinks that makes us to like him, but this is not so. He is a good man in his way, though. He truly cares for the daughter and she is not even really his."

"A rich man, you say?"

"Sí, Mr. Man." She tugged at him, trying again to get him to hurry.

"Where's he live? What does he do t' make him rich? Does he keep his money in the house?"

Still naked but obviously unconcerned about it, Anselma shrugged, got up, and sat on one of her two chairs.

"I want t' know everything you can tell me about this rich man. Where does he live?"

Anselma sighed. She was going to be late. But she did

like those beads. And if the man liked her, there might well be more beads and other pretty things in her future.

"He has a house. . . . I show you. When I leave I go there, yes? You watch. Then will you know."

"How does he make his money?" Erv prompted. He was beginning to become excited but in a way that had nothing to do with any woman.

Again she shrugged. "This is important?"

"Damn right it is. I want to know more about this man."

"It is something to do with the money, I think. Not bank, but . . . When I go there I will walk past where he works. There is a sign. I will show you."

Erv grinned and leaned forward, full of a growing excitement now.

Anselma sat answering Ederle's questions until it was time for her to dress and run lest she be late for her employment watching over young Louise Taylor.

* * *

"Listen," Erv said, leaning over the counter. He glanced around furtively and lowered his voice. "I came into some money. Sold out my whole outfit, see, an' I been looking to invest it so's I won't just blow the poke. You see what I'm saying?"

The bank teller nodded and cleared his throat. "We have excellent savings opportunities here, friend. We pay three-quarters of a percent interest and—"

"No, no, no," Erv interrupted. "What I'm thinking is a proper investment, see. An' what I been wondering is about that fella that has a sign over the dry goods store. Says he's an investment broker. I was thinking maybe you could tell me somethin' about him."

"Mr. Hahn? Oh yes, we certainly know him. He is a very good man. Very honest. Why, he handles all of this bank's investment capital." The teller was obviously not as interested as he had been, now that he knew the bank would not be getting the gentleman's money and therefore knew as well that he would not be getting a pat on the back from Mr. Bonner for bringing new business in. But he was agreeable. He always liked to help folks, that being simple Christian duty and he being a Christian.

Ederle looked puzzled. "What d'you mean he handles the bank's money? Doesn't the bank handle its own money?"

The teller laughed. But then so few lay people really understood banks and banking. "Banks don't just take in money and let it sit in vaults, you know. Money has to be put to work if you want it to grow. Banks make loans. To farmers for seed, to businesses for goods, to cattlemen for improved stock, to all manner of people for all manner of needs. The people who receive those loans return the money with interest. So a bank's capital is constantly moving in and out. It isn't allowed to just sit. And if there is a surplus of deposits, which we are proud to say we have, the excess is put to work elsewhere. That is what Mr. Hahn does for us. He takes our excess capital and invests it on our behalf." He laughed. "Or I should say on behalf of the depositors who entrusted us with it to begin with."

"I'll be damned," Ederle exclaimed. "I never knew all that. So this Hahn fellow handles all of your . . . excess, did you call it?"

"That's right." The teller smiled.

"Thank you." Ederle turned. The teller called him back.

"If you contact Mr. Hahn about taking you on as a

client, would you mind mentioning that I recommended him to you? My name is Adams." He pointed to a small plaque placed over his window. "Carl Adams. Mr. Hahn knows me."

Erv smiled. "Yeah. Yeah, I'll sure do that, Carl."

Erv was feeling very good when he exited Thom's Valley's bank.

Just think. That little man handled all of the bank's money. What did Carl say? All of the "excess" money. My, oh my. Erv grinned to himself as he walked down the block to where he had left his horse.

And he had a kid. Pretty little wife—Erv had seen her this morning when she left the house to go shopping— yes, sir, a kid and a pretty wife. And all that money. Now, wasn't that just a combination to warm a fellow's heart?

Erv laughed out loud. Warm his heart or, more to the point, his purse strings.

Yes, sir, this whole thing was coming together just fine.

Chapter 3

John Taylor laid a penny on the counter, lifted off the lid of the big apothecary jar, and withdrew two red-and-white-striped peppermint sticks.

"For Loozy?" the storekeeper said.

"One of 'em," Taylor said with a wink and a grin. He slipped one of the candies into his shirt pocket. The other he popped into his mouth, biting down until the peppermint stick crunched and crumbled.

"You're supposed to suck on those things, you know," Edmund Jewett observed.

Taylor's grin flashed again. "Was I you, Mr. Jewett, I'd encourage folks to bite them. They don't last so long and you're likely to sell more."

Jewett chuckled. "If you say so, John." He wiped his hands on his apron and reached for a feather duster.

Taylor took another bite of his candy and asked, "I don't suppose you'd have any work you need done, do you?"

"Not right now but you know I'll keep you in mind when I do need something. You always do a good job. Don't overcharge neither like some folks I know. Not that I'm saying anything about who, you understand." Jewett began dusting the shelves behind him.

"No, sir, I wouldn't expect you to." John stuck what was left of his peppermint back into his mouth, gave Jewett a bit of a wave, which the storekeeper did not see, and sauntered out onto the sidewalk, his heels ringing hollow on the rough planks. He gave thought to a shave and a haircut but settled instead for dropping into one of the rocking chairs that sat in front of Jewett's mercantile and idly watching the world—or such of it as could be found in Thom's Valley—pass by.

Gradually, slowly, Taylor's chin sank down toward his chest and his eyes drooped nearly shut. He could feel the heat of the late afternoon sun on his legs. He gave fleeting thought to buying himself a proper dinner for a change. He had enough money put by that he did not have to work for the next few days if he chose, and a meal at the café might be just the thing.

It was early for dinner, but he was feeling a mite peckish. So why not treat himself to some proper, sit-down cooking? Steak covered thick with flour gravy, say. And mashed spuds with more of the same poured over. Hot baking soda biscuits with butter and preserves and maybe some pie to finish off. Taylor had not had a meal like that since the last time he worked out at one of the larger ranches. That would have been . . . He had to think about it for a moment in order to remember. The Bar 7 H? He thought so. Not that it mattered. But the food. Oh Lord, the cook at the Bar 7 H could really put on a feed.

Taylor's mouth was watering before he got off his chair and stepped down into the street.

The next thing he knew, there was a flurry of motion to the right just outside his line of vision and he felt something smack hard on the side of his jaw.

"You son of a bitch!" someone bawled, and hit him again.

"Now damn it, you . . . Hahn?" John could scarcely believe his eyes. It was Richard Hahn who had attacked him without warning. And was doing his level best to do it again.

Hahn's fists were flying—inexpertly to be sure but every once in a while one would connect and the damn things stung when they landed—and his face was red as a dance hall girl's skirts. John could not be sure, but it almost looked like the little bastard had been crying.

Hahn tried to belt him again. John decided he had had just about enough of that. He took hold of one of Hahn's arms, spun him around, and wrapped his arms around the little man, pinning Hahn's arms firmly to his sides.

"Will you settle yourself down, you dumb shit?"

"You bastard." Hahn yelped. "You lousy son of a bitch. Where are they? What have you done with them?"

"Done with what? Man, I dunno what you're talking about."

"Let me go, damn you." Now Hahn was crying. Taylor could hear it in his voice.

"I'll let you go when you settle your ass down an' tell me what this is all about." By way of demonstration, John clamped down on Hahn even harder. He had broken a man's ribs in a bear hug once. He considered trying to duplicate that now with Richard Hahn. It would be a pleasure.

"Let me go, you big ape. I . . . I can't breathe." Hahn struggled, trying to break loose from Taylor's hold, but that was a losing proposition.

"If I let you go, will you tell me what this is about?" There was silence for a moment, so Taylor shook him a little and tried again.

Passersby were staring but no one interfered. For one thing, everyone in town knew there was bad blood between the two men. For another, there were few in the valley who wanted to tangle with John Taylor.

"Tell me what it is you want, damn you, but first you

tell me what you've done with Jessica and Loozy. Where are they? What have you done with them?"

Taylor felt a chill of sudden dread shoot through him. "What do you mean, man? They're not at home? Where are they?"

"I thought . . . oh Jesus!"

Without reaching a conscious decision, Taylor let go of Hahn. The smaller man staggered, turned around, and slumped down onto the edge of the sidewalk. He sat with his head down, openly weeping now.

"What are you talking about?" Taylor demanded.

"Jessica . . . Loozy . . . they're gone."

"Gone. What the hell d'you mean 'gone'?"

If Hahn's blurted comment had not been so serious, Taylor might have laughed at the little man. Hahn, usually so impeccable in appearance, was sitting on the sidewalk of Thom's Valley's main street, head in his hands and eyes red and puffy and running tears, necktie askew and one point of his batwing collar crumpled and pointing off to the side. The man made a ludicrous sight. But if Jessie and Loozy really were gone . . .

Taylor knelt in front of the devastated financier and shook his shoulder. Getting no response, he shook Hahn again. Hard.

Hahn looked up and glared at him. "You took them, damn you. That's what the note said. Now where are they?"

"Note. What the hell are you talking about, asshole? I didn't write any note to anybody."

"You can call me whatever you like. I don't care. But surely Jessica did not go willingly with you. What did you do, threaten to harm Loozy if she didn't do what you said? That would be just like you, you ape. All muscle and no brain, that's you. Jessica is bound to hate you after this, you know. You can't force her to love you."

Taylor held a hand up to stop the flow of Hahn's accusation. "Whoa there, shit for brains. Back up a little. What note are you talking about?"

"Why, the note you left in the house. Your note."

"I already told you, damn it, I didn't leave no damned note, not in your house nor anyplace else."

Hahn straightened his tie and tugged at the bottom of his coat, trying to get himself back in order. "You really didn't? No note?"

Taylor shook his head.

"Then . . . who did? Who took my girls?"

"Look, let's get something straight. Those aren't your girls. They're mine and don't you be forgetting it. Mine, wedded and bedded and forever. But back t' the original point, I didn't take them anyplace and I didn't leave no note neither. What does the note say exactly?"

"I . . . I don't know."

"Somebody took your, uh, lady friend and her daughter and left you a note and you didn't bother to read it? Jeez, Hahn, you're even more of a dumb shit than I thought."

"I did so read it. That is, I . . . glanced at it. Sort of. I saw that it said something about taking Jessica and Loozy and I, um, knew it had to be you that took them. So I came . . . came looking for you." Hahn peered down toward his toes, looking about as miserable as Taylor had ever seen a human person be.

"All right, damn it, I think what you and me need t' do is to look at that note. D'you have it with you? Did you put it in your pocket?"

Hahn shook his head. "I left it . . . I think I dropped it when I ran out of the house. It must still be there."

"Then that's where you and me are going now."

"You aren't going anywhere with me, you big ox. You aren't wanted. Understand? You are not welcome in my house." Hahn looked like he was ready to aim another punch at Taylor.

"Tough shit. Welcome or not, I'm coming, Hahn, unless you're big enough an' strong enough to keep me away." Taylor stood and reaching out took hold of Hahn's arm. He pulled the smaller man to his feet and turned him to face toward his house on the side of town opposite John Taylor's. "Let's go, damn you." Taylor started marching in that direction. Richard Hahn had little choice but to go along. Either that or be dragged, for he was much easier to mug than a thousand-pound longhorn steer.

* * *

Practically no one in Thom's Valley locked their doors. Except for Richard Hahn and a very few others. There were some—Taylor was not among them—who mocked the little man for that. This time the door not only was unlocked, it stood wide open to any chicken, duck, or stray cur that might wander in. Taylor followed Hahn inside. Habit made him remove his hat when he passed through the doorway.

Taylor had never been inside Jessie's current home. It was pretty much what he expected. Small but impeccably furnished. All cherrywood and chintz, with frames on the walls and pillows on the couch and chairs. And it was tidy. Jessica liked to keep things in order. Taylor liked that but did not bother with it now that she was gone. The house smelled of lilac water and naphtha soap. It smelled like his shack used to.

"Here. Right here." Hahn plucked a half sheet of foolscap off the arm of an overstuffed easy chair. He read the note, blurted "Jesus!" and showed it to Taylor.

> I GOT YOU WIFE AN KID.
> YOU WANT THEM BACK PAY THE BANK MONEY ALL OF IT.
> I HAVE TWO MEN OF MY GANG WATCHING YOU. YOU GO TO THE MARSHEL OR SHERFF AND THEY DIE GURANTEE THEY DIE.
> I GIVE YOU TWO WEEK TO PAY ME. I WILL SEND YOU NOTE TO TELL HOW & WHERE TO PAY ME MY MONEY.
> REMEMBER. YOU ARE BEING WATCH. NO FALSE MOVE OR BOTH DIE. REMEMBER.

"Jesus!" Taylor echoed Hahn's exclamation.

Hahn crumpled the paper and threw it down. Taylor bent over and retrieved it. He smoothed the sheet over his thigh and walked aimlessly around the parlor.

"I still think you had something to do with this," Hahn said, his voice unsteady.

"You want proof that I didn't? I can give you proof, you idiot." Taylor stopped and whirled to face Hahn.

Hahn glared at him without speaking.

"Read the damn note again. It says something about your 'wife.' Which Jessie never was an' never will be. I wouldn't've wrote it like that if it was me. Besides, my English ain't that bad. Mine ain't perfect but it sure isn't that bad."

"I'm being watched, it says. They will harm Jessica and Louise if I go to the marshal or one of the sheriff's deputies."

Taylor resumed his pacing, fists clenched at his side. "Being watched? Being watched by who? Do you know?"

"Let me see that note again." Hahn held his hand out.

Taylor hesitated for a moment, then handed it over. They were silent as Hahn spent several long moments rereading the kidnap note.

"Two men, it says."

"Could be anybody," Taylor said. "Have you noticed strangers in town?"

"No, but then I wouldn't necessarily notice anyone. I mean . . . people come and go all the time. I don't pay all that much attention to . . . that sort."

"And what sort would that be?" Taylor challenged.

Hahn met his eye, chin defiantly up. "Your low-life sort," he answered.

Taylor's complexion darkened, but he contained his fury. For the moment.

Hahn walked across the room to one of the front windows and stared out of it; then without breaking his gaze from whatever he was looking at he said, "I can't tell."

"What the hell are you talking about now?"

"The note. Somebody watching. I can't tell. There could be someone on the street or something. Someone watching my office."

"Could you really take all the bank's money and turn it over to these people? If you had to, I mean." Taylor came over to the window too. He stood beside Hahn and looked out at what he could see of the town.

Hahn hesitated, then looked at Taylor. He took a deep breath. His shoulders slumped and his expression was haggard. He nodded. "Yes. If I had to," he said slowly, as if having to drag each word out kicking and screaming against exposure.

"How the hell could you do a thing like that?"

"I have power of attorney for the investment funds. I could . . . I could go down to Pueblo and take it all out in cash. A lot of it anyway. Anything past a certain point and they would need authorization from the bank. But I could get . . . a lot. They would give it to me, I'm sure. I could . . . Jessica is dear to me, Taylor. You can't know how much. I would do anything to protect her." His voice dropped to a whisper. "Anything."

Taylor stood where he was for several seconds, then said, "I want something to drink, damn it. You got anything to drink in this house?"

"Sit down. I'll get something. I could use a drink too." Hahn turned and went into the kitchen.

Taylor paused, then deliberately took a seat in the easy chair that he was sure would be Richard Hahn's usual resting place.

* * *

Taylor felt a pang of deep hurt when Hahn returned to the room carrying a fancy silver tray with a cut glass decanter on it and a pair of matching tumblers. The set was Jessica's. Taylor had given it to her the Christmas before Loozy was born. Jess saw the set in a mail-order catalog and fell in love with it. John saved every extra penny for four months in order to buy it for her. Now . . .

He glared at Hahn, who almost certainly had no idea what the set meant to Jessie. Or to Taylor.

"We have to get them back," Hahn said as he poured a stiff drink and handed the glass to Taylor.

It took John a moment to remember what the man was talking about. His concentration had been on the silver tray and drink set. "I dunno what you think you and me can do. The note says you're being watched. Likely I am by now too. We can't go to the law. Maybe nothing would happen if we did, but maybe the bastards would see that an' do . . . what they said they'd do." The very thought of it made him cringe. Jessie. Louise. They were both so sweet, so very dear. Now . . .

"It takes a low son of a bitch to threaten harm to a woman and a child." There was venom in Hahn's voice.

Taylor sent a sharp look toward the man. He hadn't been sure the prissy son of a bitch knew that sort of language. Probably hadn't used words like that since he was a pimple-faced kid reading penny dreadfuls in the outhouse. Thinking of which . . .

Taylor set his glass aside and stood.

"You aren't leaving, are you?" Hahn sounded close to panic. As much as he despised John Taylor, he was clearly leaning on the man now.

"I got t' take a leak."

"Oh. Sorry. Uh, the crapper is—"

"I know where it is well enough. I put the stovepipe through your kitchen roof." He hesitated, then reminded himself that he did not owe Richard Asshole Hahn a damn thing. Not one damn thing. "Of course that was when Paul Hicken lived here. Back before you went an' stole my wife."

"Jessica is . . . ," Hahn began to protest, but there was no point. His voice died away to nothing as Taylor was not listening to him.

Taylor was already on his way through the passageway into the kitchen where he could still smell the lingering scents of Jessica's cooking. His stomach rumbled sourly, but that was not from anything having to do with food; he was filled with fear for both Jessica and Loozy. He could not lose them again. Not this way.

There had to be something that could be done to get them safely back, even if that something took every penny of every man, woman, and child in Thom's Valley.

Jessica Taylor

Jessica moaned softly through clenched teeth. She did not want the ugly old bastard to hear. And yes, she did know those words. She had never in her life used them, but she knew them all right. And this right here was a time to be thinking them at the very least.

They had been riding for . . . she did not know how long but it seemed a very long time. Hours, she guessed. She despised having to ride anyway and to do it like this—blindfolded and with her hands bound tight to the saddle horn—was worse yet. Her thighs ached to the point of real pain and she had to pee something awful. Every time the stupid horse took a step, her bladder felt like it would burst.

"Whoa."

The horse stopped. She could feel the animal behind hers, the one Loozy was riding, move up close and nudge the back of her right thigh. Her dress had hiked up so that she could straddle the animal, and now its nose, soft and velvety, touched bare flesh. That was not so bad, but its whiskers were prickly.

"Set there just a minute," the old man said in a perfectly ordinary tone. "I'll come untie you pretty soon."

Jess heard movement and crackling sounds in some dry brush and then there was a glimmer of light around the edges of her blindfold. The old bastard must have lighted a lamp or started a fire.

"You first, little girl." His voice came from behind but not far. Beside Loozy's horse, she supposed.

"My name is Louise!" Loozy snapped. She sounded more annoyed than frightened. "And I am not a little girl."

Jessica heard more movement and then a heartfelt sigh. Loozy was down off her horse, Jess surmised. A few moments later she felt the man fumbling at the cords that bound her to the saddle. The bonds fell away and the man said, "You can get down now."

"I can't see."

"You want to be waited on or something? Your hands ain't tied now. Take you own damn blind off."

"I'm allowed to do that?" She did not want to make him any angrier than he already seemed to be. He really was a horrid thing.

"Sure. Ain't nothing here to see but rocks an' dirt."

Jessica tugged away the rag that was serving as a blindfold—a rather smelly rag at that—to discover they were at the bottom of some sort of gully or small canyon. Certainly they were nowhere that she recognized, but then she almost never left town and then only in a coach.

She crawled painfully down from the horse and braced herself on legs that were shaky to the point that she was afraid she might fall down. She took hold of the stirrup leather beside her for stability and gave herself a moment to recover.

Loozy came rushing up from behind and attached herself to Jessica's waist as firmly as a leech. The child buried herself against her mother's side and clung for all she was worth.

The man, old and bearded and frightening with those guns and knives and whatnot hanging on and around him, was holding a collapsible miner's lantern with a candle burning behind the glass panes. That was all the light there was and it was none too bright. The glass looked like it had not been cleaned since the lantern left wherever it was made.

In his other hand the man held a nearly empty burlap sack. He held it out, offering it to Jess.

"What's this?" Her nose wrinkled with distaste at the thought of what such a filthy creature might carry on his person.

"Supper," he said. "Biscuits that I brung from town."

"I want something more than cold biscuits," Jessica snapped with a toss of her chin. A very pretty chin. Everyone said so. Men always gave Jessica what she asked.

The man shrugged. "You don't wanta eat, it ain't no skin off my ass." He opened the bag, took out a biscuit, and began to munch, crumbs dribbling down the front of his shirt.

Jessica drew herself up to her full height and said, "I will thank you to mind your language in front of my daughter."

"Miz Hahn, you can want whatever the hell you want, but you might wanta keep in mind who's the boss here. An' it ain't you." The ugly old thing shoved the remainder of that biscuit into his mouth. His cheeks bulged slightly from being so full. Chipmunk cheeks, Jessica thought.

Jess took Loozy by the hand and tugged her off toward a bush of some sort that she could see at the edge of the lamplight.

"Just where the hell d'you think you're goin'?" the man demanded.

Jessica snorted and tossed her head. "A gentleman does not inquire of a lady at a time like this."

"Maybe not, but I'm no damn gen'leman and you ain't going nowhere 'less I say so." He took hold of the haft of the huge knife that hung from his belt. "Try anything, lady, and I'll cut your tits off."

"We have to pee-pee," Loozy piped up quickly, rotating her face away from her mama's side just long enough to get the words out before she again buried herself against Jessica's side.

"Hell, why didn't you say so? All right. Go. But don't neither one o' you go no fu'ther than that bush yonder. Try that an' I'll hear an' it won't go easy on you after. You understand me?"

Jessica nodded. She could feel Loozy nod as well.

"All right, then. Go 'head." He motioned impatiently for them to proceed.

Jess had never been so miserable in her life. She was tired, she was hurting, and she was frightened half to death. And she had to pee something awful.

All she could do was to hope the marshal or the sheriff or somebody would come soon to rescue them.

"Come on, baby," she said, "but watch out for snakes and wild animals and things." She peeled Loozy away from her side and held on to her hand, leading the way into the bushes.

Chapter 4

Taylor set his glass aside, the contents barely touched. He leaned his head back against the upholstery of Hahn's easy chair, closed his eyes, and stayed like that for several moments. Then he sat up, looked at Richard Hahn, and said, "We have to get them back."

"Yes, of course, but the note says we don't dare go to the law. The kidnappers will see. They will kill Jessica and Loozy. The note says they are watching."

"Watching you maybe. It didn't say anything about me. Whoever wrote that note thinks Jess is your wife. They must not know about me. Might be watching the town marshal maybe, but I can get around that. I can ride over to Cauley an' get the sheriff to look for them. Whoever the bastards are they oughta be hung." He grunted. "An' I'd be glad to tie the noose."

"You can't do that. You can't go see the sheriff any more than I can," Hahn said. He looked like he was close to tears again. "Try to think, man. They don't have to actually see either one of us talking to the marshal or the sheriff. If they see a posse, they'll know the law has been tipped. That might be enough to put Jessica and Loozy in danger."

"But we don't actually know—"

"I said 'might.' Do you want to take a chance with their lives? Is that what you want, you fool?"

"You know I don't, but—"

"We are not going to call the law in on this," Hahn said emphatically.

"All right. Fine. You don't wanta talk to the sheriff, then pay them their damn ransom money. Anything to get Jess and Loozy back safe and sound."

Hahn tossed back the rest of his brandy and replaced the empty glass onto the silver tray. He got up and began pacing around the room. "I can't give them the money."

"Can't?" Taylor's voice hardened. "Or won't?"

"Mustn't," Hahn said. "What would happen to the people of this town if suddenly they had no money? That is not the bank's money, you know. It belongs to all the depositors who entrusted the bank with it. And the bank has given me their trust. Why, it would ruin Thom's Valley if I gave all the money to a gang of kidnappers. The whole damn town would be bankrupt. We wouldn't exist any longer. Not as a community anyway."

"Fine. We can all start over someplace else. I don't care. I just want my wife and daughter back."

Hahn stopped pacing and glared at him. "Jessica is not yours any longer, Taylor. Get that through your thick head."

"We can quarrel over Jess later on, you piece of shit," he snapped. "Right now I just wanta get them safe."

"So do I, but I will not ruin this community. I just . . . I just can't do such a thing."

"Not even for Jess?"

"Don't put it like that. It is not an 'either-or' proposition. Yes, we have to get the girls back. No, we cannot ruin Thom's Valley to do it. We have to find another way."

"Good luck," Taylor said sarcastically. "Give me another drink, damn it." He still had a nearly full glass, but Hahn tipped the decanter over it and topped off the contents. Taylor tossed that off, sat, and again tipped his head back with his eyes closed. "I dunno about you," he mumbled, "but I've had better days than this'un."

* * *

Taylor sat up and glared at Hahn. "Give them the damn money, you tightwad son of a bitch."

Hahn glared right back but otherwise ignored him.

"Do something, damn you!" Taylor shouted. "It's Jessie's life we're talking about here. And little Loozy. You might not care so much about her, but—"

Taylor hardly had time for the words to leave his mouth before Hahn was out of his chair and charging forward, fists balled and eyes half crazed. He stopped short of the physical attack, however, and soon shrank back on the sofa. "Do not presume," he hissed, "to tell me what I feel. I love that little girl like she was my very own."

"Well, she ain't yours, you bastard. Not any more'n Jessie is. They're the both of them mine. My wife, my daughter. See that you understand that, mister."

Hahn turned away rather than continue the dispute. For lack of any better idea he picked up the brandy decanter, poured himself another drink, and set the bottle down again without offering any to Taylor. He left the drink on the tray and began pacing about the room.

After a few moments Taylor stood and began pacing as well. He stopped short halfway around the parlor. He stood staring at an ornate polished silver frame holding a photograph of a threesome: Jessica Taylor, Richard Hahn, and, between the two of them, young Louise Taylor in her prettiest party dress. It was all too obviously a "family" view with a bucolic pasture scene on the canvas drop behind the three of them.

The photo took Taylor's breath away. He had given that frame to Jessie. A family photo had indeed been in it but showing Loozy—only five at the time if he remembered correctly—between Jessica and himself. The backdrop was even the same in that picture. The backdrop still hung in George Moorhaus's photographic studio over in Cauley or at least had been there the last time he passed by. The painting was there in plain view from the front windows where Moorhaus's latest photos were always displayed. There had been a time when the Taylor family portrait hung there for all to see. The Taylor family, not this monstrosity. John Taylor looked at the photo and remembered what had been and he ached. His gut churned and he remembered. Oh God, he remembered. His eyes burned and he felt like joining Hahn in tears. It was all he could do to maintain control.

Damn Hahn anyway. And damn those kidnappers. If Jessie hadn't run off with this prissy son of a bitch, she would be safe now. At home fixing his dinner. At home where she belonged. Safe.

* * *

"Give me a drink."

"Get it yourself." Hahn sounded as thoroughly miserable as Taylor felt. As thoroughly drunk too.

Taylor reached for the bottle, missed, tried again. He did not bother with a glass but drank straight from the bottle. Hahn took the bottle from him and he too drank from it.

The brandy decanter had long since been emptied and put aside. A whiskey bottle followed and now it was nearly empty. The two men were bleary-eyed and wobbly, their senses fuddled with drink.

"Got to get 'em back," Taylor said.

Hahn bobbed his head in agreement. "Got to."

"My wife," Taylor said. "My kid."

Hahn grunted but did not bother to refute the claim.

"Bastard," Taylor snarled.

Hahn pretended not to know who Taylor was talking about when he said that.

"Get them."

"Yes. Got to," Hahn said.

"Tomorrow. Get the damn money. Give it to them."

"I'd go to jail."

"Who gives a shit?"

"Can't go to jail. Ruin everything. Gonna be big man someday. Rich. Governor maybe. Big, big man."

"You'd let Jessie be killed so you can be governor, you bastard?"

"Anyway, can't get that much money."

"You said you could."

"That was . . . technically maybe I could. Been thinking, though. It wouldn't"—Hahn belched—"wouldn't work. The bank would need . . . would need ap . . . approval from Randy Bonner. He wouldn't . . . sure he wouldn't agree without, um, knowing why. Been thinking. And anyway don't want to go to jail. No, got to go find them and get them back."

"From a whole gang of armed men?"

Hahn nodded solemnly. "Yes. From the whole stinking, son-of-a-bitch gang."

"The hell you say!"

"The hell I don't." Hahn slid down onto the floor, stretched out, and within seconds was peacefully asleep. John Taylor shrugged and reached for the whiskey bottle. Hahn might be a son of a bitch, he reflected, but the man bought good whiskey.

Louise Taylor

If she weren't so frightened, this would be terribly romantic. How was it that the fairy tales she loved to read failed to tell what was really so? She was supposed to be enchanted by a handsome brigand. Instead the huge man was ugly and scary and, well, smelly. He smelled sour and sweaty and filthy dirty. She knew she was close to him when he blindfolded her and put her onto the horse and tied her hands to the saddle horn thing.

This was no fairy tale and the man was no Prince Charming.

Loozy was mounted on the last horse in the procession, the farthest away from the man. If she managed to get her hands loose from the saddle and to slip down to the ground, the man might not notice for, she hoped, miles and miles.

She could hide in the bushes and find her way back to town and everyone would say what a hero she was to give the alarm and then Daddy would go and rescue Mama and things would be all right again. They would be a family again, the way it used to be.

Dick was nice enough. She even sort of liked him. But Daddy was, well, Daddy. Daddy teased her and he played with her and he loved her. Really, really loved her. She knew that. And she knew he would come for her. No matter what and no matter where, he would come for her.

In the meantime she had to think about getting loose

so she could go tell the town and, more important, tell
Daddy and he would ride out and find the man and get
Mama back and, oh, things would be right and good and
fun once again.

Chapter 5

"Good Lord, Taylor. What are you doing here?" Dick Hahn rolled onto his side and struggled into a sitting position. He was on the floor in his own parlor. His head was throbbing and his mouth felt like it was packed with cotton wool. Used cotton wool. "Jesus," he blurted, the name a rarity coming from his dry lips.

"D' you say somethin'?" Taylor looked to be in little better condition than Dick was this morning. His hair was wildly disarranged and he needed a shave, but he did not look to be as gut-sour as Dick felt at that particular moment.

Morning. Right. So it was. There was strong sunlight streaming through the front window. Jessica's tray and cut glass decanter were sitting on the coffee table. That was all right. But there was a whiskey bottle—empty it appeared—lying on the rug between Dick and John Taylor. Taylor was stretched out on the sofa, his boots hanging over at one end and his greasy hair propped on one of Jessica's lovely pillows. Taylor looked as befuddled as Dick felt. But then to Dick the ignoramus always looked like a big, befuddled, dumb brute.

The man sat up, swayed just a little—Dick could well imagine how dizzy he must be—and mumbled, "What th' hell 'm I doing here?"

"That's what I just asked."

The man shook his head, tried to stand up but thought

better of that, and settled back onto the sofa. "Tied one on last night, did'n we?"

"Yes." Dick mouthed the vile fruits of a night of drinking, licked his lips, and then observed, "Yes, I would say that we did."

"Didn't accomplish much, did we?"

"No, I would say we did not."

Taylor stood, almost fell but righted himself. "Where's your whiskey? I need a hair o' the dog."

"I think we drank it all last night. There was only the one bottle in the house." He pointed to the empty that was lying on the floor between them. "I think that was it."

"Ain't that just hell? Rich man like you an' he only has one bottle in the place. Ain't that the shits?"

"Last night," Dick said slowly, trying to think past the fog that invaded his brain and made his thoughts fuzzy and indistinct. "Last night we talked about getting Jessica and Louise back where they belong. Didn't we?"

"Yeah. We did. We need t' get them back where they belong. Which is with me, by the way. They're my family, not yours."

"Never mind that," Dick snapped. "This isn't a time to be arguing about who belongs where. Whoever they belong to, they are in grave danger. The note says they will be killed if we tell the marshal or call in the sheriff and his deputies. So how are we going to get them back? And don't tell me to pay the ransom. You know I can't do that. Even if I wanted to, and I have mixed feelings about that, I couldn't."

Taylor ignored Dick's comment. "You got anything to eat in this house?"

"How can you think about food at a time like this?" The very thought was enough to make Dick want to puke.

Right at that moment food would be just about the last thing on his mind.

"I think better on a full stomach," Taylor said, yawning. He made a face, scratched his belly, and sat down again.

"If we have anything . . . I don't know. Jessie always took care of things like that." Dick fluttered his hands in futility.

"Come on, then. We'll go over to the café and get something. Maybe a hair of the dog after we eat."

"No drinking. No more until we get the girls back," Dick said.

Taylor gave him a dirty look. "Who died an' made you boss?" he demanded.

"It's just . . . we need to keep our heads clear from now on. If you don't want to help me, though, just say so. I'll go get them on my own."

Taylor snorted derisively. "Go where? Get them how?"

"I haven't figured that out yet. We'll talk about it after breakfast."

Taylor looked around, spotted his hat lying upside down on a chair, and retrieved it. "Ready?"

Dick felt grubby. He desperately needed to change his underthings and put on a fresh shirt. Taylor did not seem to care about such things. The hell with it, Dick thought. He pulled his wrinkled suit coat over his belly and buttoned it, that being all the sartorial preparation he made for the day. "Let's go," he said.

* * *

Dick carefully buttered a bit of biscuit, spooned a tiny portion of wild strawberry jam onto the biscuit, and ate it. He peered across the table with distaste at the sight of Taylor wolfing down a plate of pork chops and fried potatoes. The oaf had no manners whatsoever. Dick could not for the life of him understand why sweet, delicate, ladylike Jessica agreed to marry the man in the first place. The day when a divorce was granted and Dick was free to make Jessica his wife could not arrive too soon.

Jessica Hahn, Mrs. Richard Hahn, those had a very nice sound, he thought.

Soon. Just as soon as they could get Taylor out of their lives. Well, mostly out. The man would always be Louise's father and Dick would never knowingly do anything to hurt Loozy. He could not care for that little girl any more if she were his own flesh and blood.

Blood! God, the thought of Jessica and Loozy being harmed by that horrid gang of cutthroats . . . if he could he would be tempted to steal from the bank and pay the vicious bastards their ransom.

It did not escape Dick's attention that he could steal some of the bank's investment funds and palm that off as the total. Surely the gang would not know how much of the bank's capital was placed for investment.

Or could they?

Might they have someone actually inside the bank who already told them what to expect and how it could be gotten? That was not impossible, he supposed. They could have bribed one of the bank's employees to provide them with that information. For that matter, a bank employee might well be a member of the gang.

He had not seen the actual books, of course, but he had a sense of the bank's finances. He knew there was not a great deal of money allocated to employee salaries. One of them might be tempted to steal, especially if they were in financial straits. Gambling debt. A note coming due. Something on that order of things.

No, it was not impossible. Improbable, true, but not

impossible. And would he want to wager Jessica's life on it? Never. He sighed.

Dick's head was hurting. And not just from last night's excessive drinking.

If only he knew what to do.

"Pass me that ketchup, would'ja?"

Dick pushed the slim green bottle closer to Taylor and watched the man drown his fried potatoes in the stuff. Hahn did not much like ketchup. Did not much like John Taylor either for that matter. He returned his attention to the platter of biscuits and bowl of freshly churned sweet butter.

What to do? Damn it, what to do?

* * *

"By now they know that you and me are talking," Taylor said. "The note didn't say anything about that and if they don't like it, well, too damn bad. Jess surely will've told them that she has both a husband and a boyfriend, so we oughta get away with this much, but we sure can't call in the law."

"That states the problem," Dick said, picking his teeth with a sliver of aspen wood that he pried off the side of the bench they were sitting on. "It does nothing to come up with a solution. If you can't do any better than that, then I—"

"Slow the hell down, will you? I'm thinking."

"I didn't know you could," Dick snapped.

"Maybe better'n you think I can, asshole."

Dick started to bristle, but Taylor settled him down with a show of his palm in a "stop" motion. "What I was gonna say," Taylor said slowly, "is that you an' me got to go after them."

Dick gave him a look of sharp impatience. "Are you out of your damned mind, Taylor? Of course we have to bring them back. But just where in blue blazes are we supposed to look for them? Do you know where they've been taken? Do you have any earthly idea where we should start looking?"

Taylor shook his head. He settled back on the bench in front of the barbershop and crossed his legs. "'Course I don't know. But I'm thinking we might could get a hint or two."

"How are we supposed to do that?"

"Mister, I've trailed lost cows half my life. Deer, elk, all them. I know how to follow a trail."

"What trail do you have it in mind to follow, cowboy?" Dick sneered.

"Don't got one yet, o' course, but think about it. They won't've rode the stagecoach outta town. Aren't likely to've showed themselves out on the public roads neither. Which means they likely cut back toward the mountains." He gestured over his shoulder in the general direction of the snowcapped peaks that lay to the west, far higher than the relatively tame mountains that were situated east of Thom's Valley.

"Why that direction?" Dick asked.

"'Cause it's the quickest way to get outta sight. Once they get up into the hills, they can't be seen from the flats. Once they get into those mountains, they can lose themselves for months at a time. Over that way"—he pointed to the east—"there's folks moving around. Running cows and sheep and such. No, sir, to them mountains west of here. That's sure the way I'd head if I wanted to hide somebody I wasn't supposed to have hold of."

"All right, let's say you can find a trail. Then what?"

Dick was still skeptical, all the more so because it was John Taylor who was proposing the plan.

Taylor's eyes glinted and his lips compressed to a thin line. "Then we kill the sons of bitches."

Dick supposed that he should object to that comment. He did not.

* * *

"I'm gonna go borrow me a horse from the livery an' start scouting around. It's best to do that before the sun gets too high." Dick seemed to be puzzled, so Taylor added, "When the sun is shinin' on a slant, it causes shadows, makes it easier to spot tracks."

"Oh. I . . . suppose that makes sense. You don't have a horse? I see you riding through town all the time."

"Mister, you got a lot to learn. A working hand has got no business owning his own horse. They're convenient but they have to be sheltered and fed whether they're earning their keep or not. Cowhands ride the horses of whatever outfit they happen to be working for."

"I never knew that."

"There's a lot o' things you don't know, Hahn." Taylor scowled, then said, "While I'm gone you'd best get us some supplies. You can say . . . hell, I dunno. You're the liar, not me. Make something up. Just make sure nobody ends up wondering what we're up to. You got any guns?"

"Shotguns," Dick admitted.

"You got a spare that I can carry?" Taylor asked.

"Yes, I have my everyday shotgun and I have a rather special custom gun too. You don't have a gun? No kind of gun?"

"Mister, I do odd jobs around town that I need a hammer an' saw for and I do day work with cows. For them I need a saddle and a rope. But I don't need a gun for any of it."

"That surprises me. I always thought—"

"Never mind all the shit you've thought that isn't so. Are both your shotguns the same size?"

Hahn nodded. "They're both twelve gauge."

"Fine," Taylor said. "Get a bunch of shells for that size. Couple boxes anyway. Single-ought buck would be good. You can say you're going deer hunting with some fellas from over in Cauley. One thing, though."

"What's that?"

"I don't got much money. You'll have to foot the bill."

Dick's chin lifted and he looked Taylor straight in the eye. "This is for Jessica. I don't care if it takes every cent I have."

Taylor held his gaze for several moments that seemed much longer than they really were. Then he turned toward the door. "I'm gonna see can I pick up that trail. I'll meet you back here in a couple hours. Soon as I find something, whenever that is."

Ervin Ederle

Damned women, Erv Ederle grumbled half aloud as his horse stumbled and slid down a rocky, brush-strewn chute.

"Please. Stop. You really must let us get off. It's too . . . we'll fall. I don't trust these animals and my limbs ache quite abominably. Please let us get down for a little while."

Damned women, Erv repeated under his breath. They were bad enough at most times, but women who could not even cook were worse than useless.

He would show this one, though. She would learn to cook a proper meal for him or he would take a cinch strap to her butt. Better yet, he would strap the kid. That ought to make her hop.

Damn kids too. This one was all the time leaking, running snot from her nose and tears from her eyes until she was all swole up so bad he could hardly tell what she properly looked like. Useless little bitch, just like her mother.

At least they soon would be at his hidey-hole. Another couple days would have them there. The place likely was a prospect hole where some fool miner looked for mineral and came up empty. Idiot dug deep enough before he quit, though. Through solid rock too. Erv could not understand the sort of man who would go to all that bother for a few pennies of gold or silver when there was so much of the stuff lying about practically free for the taking.

He smiled to himself at the thought of the payout he was fixing to put in his saddlebags.

How much was a bank worth? Five thousand? Ten? A man could live high on the hog for the rest of his days with that kind of money in his poke. Buy himself a little brown-skinned Mex girl. Two. Hell, a dozen if he wanted them. Live high and easy with all the cerveza and beans a man could want. Ah, that would be the life. A Yankee with money in his pockets? Why, he would be a big man in all the ways that mattered, so he would.

And all he had to do to get it was to sit back laughing and scratching and wait for the dumb broad's husband to bring it to him.

He would keep them alive, though. Just in case he had to show the husband some bona fides.

Once the rich bastard turned over the money, well, that was a different story. He wouldn't need any of them alive after that. Although then he could afford to be . . . what was the word . . . magnanimous. He might let them go then. Or not.

Whatever he decided, God knew he did not want to keep this stupid, complaining, no-account female. Not permanently.

Erv shook his head. Why any sane man, especially a rich one, would choose to hitch himself to a deadweight like this skinny, yellow-haired thing he simply did not understand. The kid was not all bad—almost but not quite all—but the woman, damn!

"I need to stop. I have to . . . I have to go. Really. I mean it. I'm going to go all over your saddle if you don't let me get down and do my business." The voice, that whining, incessant voice, reached him from behind.

Erv ignored the bitch, hunched his shoulders as if from a physical blow, and rode deliberately on without pause.

It wasn't his saddle anyway.

Chapter 6

Taylor opened the door and went in without knocking. He did not remove his hat once he was inside.

Hahn looked up from his easy chair and scowled. "Took your own sweet time about it, didn't you?" he grumbled. He did not stand to greet his "guest."

"I'm not quick enough for you? Fine. We can split up right here and now, mister. You gallop off in a big-assed hurry in the wrong direction whilst I take my time but get on their trail."

Hahn's expression changed to a flash of sudden hope. "You found their tracks?" This time he did come out of his chair. He crossed the room to stand in front of Taylor, both fear and hope naked in his expression.

"More or less," Taylor said.

"What is more or less supposed to mean, man? Did you find their tracks or not?"

"You don't know much about tracking, I take it. So let me explain somethin', city boy. I know cows. I know how to track down cows that have strayed. The thing is, you don't try an' find a long string o' footprints going from here to there and follow along behind them one by one. What you do is learn what cows is all about. You see just enough to figure out what direction they're moving, then you look on ahead from there. Is it the heat o' the day? If 'tis, then you look for good shade where they can lie down out of the sun and rest. First thing in the morning?

Look for water. Middle morning or late afternoon? Look for foliage for them to graze.

"Now, maybe I don't know all that much about trailing men . . . for a fact I don't," Taylor admitted, "but I figure it's bound to be sorta the same thing. Find what direction they're headed, then look out ahead to see what they might be aiming toward."

"Damn you, are you going to answer my question or not?" Hahn snapped. "Did you find tracks or didn't you?"

"I found . . . something. Likely them but there's no guarantees. For sure I found where some horses have passed."

"How many?"

"Damn it, man, give me a minute to finish what I'm saying. I don't know how many horses because they're riding single file. Without I get to know the tracks of individual horses, and without I know for certain sure that it's them, I really can't say how many nor exactly where they're headed. But this trail I did spot, it's headed into the high country, away from any graze cows ought to be using at this time o' year. That makes it all the more likely it's the bunch we want."

"And Jessica? Loozy? Can you tell if they're all right?"

Taylor gave the man a look of disgust. "Maybe you're so damned good that you can tell who's riding a horse just from looking at the tracks. Me, I can't do that."

"I read someplace," Hahn said, "that you can tell if the rider is a woman or a child by seeing how deep the hoofprint marks the ground."

Taylor snorted. "That's a bunch o' crap. How heavy is the horse?"

"What horse?"

"The horse that left this track you're telling me about. How much does this horse weigh?"

"Why . . . how could I know a thing like that?"

"Exactly. You couldn't. Neither could I."

"Oh." Hahn frowned as the meaning of Taylor's comments began to sink it.

"What I'm telling you is, maybe . . . mind now that I said maybe . . . maybe we got a direction to go in. Did you get us outfitted? Horses? Pack animal? Supplies for a long chase?"

"Yes. I did."

"Shells for those shotguns and saddle scabbards to carry 'em in?"

"Everything I thought we could need. I . . . brought what cash I could too. In case we can talk the kidnappers into taking what we can give them without ruining the town."

"All right. Change your clothes for some hunting togs an' let's go. Them downtown duds," he laughed, "they ain't gonna do well out in the hills."

"Now?" Hahn looked surprised. "Is that what you mean?"

"Hell, we could lie up an' wait a week or so if you'd rather," Taylor said sarcastically.

Hahn sighed. Then he stood and took a deep breath. "All right, Taylor. Let's get after those sons of bitches."

* * *

"How's come two packhorses, Hahn? Are you wanting to travel in comfort?"

"I got two in case Jess and Loozy need to ride them back home," Hahn explained.

"Oh, I . . . damn it, I'm a little bit embarrassed," Taylor admitted. "I shoulda thought of that my own self."

Taylor picked up and examined each foot of each horse, including the pack animals. Shoes and hooves alike appeared to be sound and healthy, and he knew for a fact that at least one of the packhorses went well under saddle because he had used the beast himself on more than one occasion when a job called for working from horseback.

Since Hahn did not seem to know to do the chore, Taylor examined Hahn's saddle mount as well, then said, "They're all sound an' ready. Reckon we can head out."

"Good enough." Hahn carefully—rather nervously, Taylor thought—checked the cinches on his rented horse and saddle, then stepped gingerly into the stirrup. The horse stood steady as a rock. With an expression of great relief, Hahn settled deeper into the saddle and flopped his heels against the brown animal's sides.

John Taylor struggled to suppress a smile.

As soon as it felt Hahn's heels, the horse exploded into a high, twisting leap.

The brown came pounding back to earth. Hahn remained hanging in midair. The horse darted sideways out from beneath him and Richard Hahn crashed to the ground in a heap. By then Taylor already had captured the loose reins of the brown and was standing nearby.

He laughed. He tried not to. He really did. But he could not help himself.

Hahn bounced up, immediately angry. Then he too found some humor in his discomfort. Grumbling, he reached out to regain the reins of the brown.

Taylor shook his head. "Nah, I'll ride this one," he said. "I've used the miserable son of a bitch in the past.

He's only spooky first time you crawl up on him in the morning. After that he makes a pretty good cow pony. This one here, though," Taylor said, pointing to his own chosen mount, "he's steady. I think maybe we'd best swap those saddles. I'll take the brown. You can have this paint. But I'm gonna ride my own saddle. You can manage with that rented thing."

Hahn gave Taylor a long, thoughtful look; then he nodded his head. "Thanks. I . . . I appreciate it." He turned away and began loosening the cinches of the livery saddle.

Taylor did not mention that he had known full well what the brown would do when Hahn tried to ride it. He told himself that he wanted to take the measure of the little man, and that was partially true. It was also true that John Taylor wanted to see Richard Hahn's scrawny ass hit the dirt when the brown horse threw him.

* * *

"Here," Taylor said, stopping his horse and pointing at the ground. "See it?"

"That little scrape, you mean?"

"That's right. That's the track I found."

"It doesn't look much like a footprint," Hahn said skeptically.

"If the kidnappers was nice enough t' walk through soft mud, I'm sure they woulda left proper hoofprints. On ground this hard a scrape is 'bout the best we can hope for. Now, that's one there. Then over here"—he leaned out of the saddle and pointed again—"over here is another. From this'un to that gives us the direction they was going. You see what I mean?"

Hahn nodded. "Yes, of course." He aimed a finger at

the nearer scrape, moved his arm so the finger pointed at the far scrape and then let his hand rise toward the horizon. "There is a . . . what would you call it, a swale? There looks to be a swale over there."

"Which is where I figure they went. Up that draw toward the mountains. I been up there. The draw turns into a shallow canyon, then peters out where a couple ridges come together."

"And that is where you expect to find them?"

"It'd be nice, but I don't 'expect' nothing. I just know I'm gonna follow wherever those sons o' bitches lead, wherever that is, however long it takes." Taylor leaned back against his cantle and scowled.

Hahn said nothing, but his expression was as grim as Taylor's as he nudged the paint horse forward again.

* * *

Richard Hahn broke a three-inch piece off the end of a juniper twig and tossed it into the fire. He watched it flare and quickly burn up, then broke off another small piece and threw it in after the first. "We didn't do very well today, did we?" he asked.

Taylor shrugged. "We got out the town. We got this far. That's something."

"But Jessica . . ."

"Is no worse off tonight than what she was this morning," Taylor said.

"What if they . . ." Hahn swallowed hard. He seemed to be having trouble getting the words out. "What if they ravage her?"

"I know you'd care, Hahn, but would that make her soiled goods to you? Would you feel different about her?" Taylor reached for a stick, wrapped some soft dough around it, and began roasting the pan bread over the coals.

"I resent that implication," Hahn snapped.

"Huh. Resent all you damn please. I still ask the question."

"I took her in after she was with you, didn't I?"

"Ain't the same thing. I was married to her. Still am, for that matter. This is different. We don't know how many kidnappers there are. They might could all pass her around among them. Loozy too, for that matter. Wouldn't make no difference to me. I love them. Both of them. I'd be happy to get them back after a hundred men was with them. But a prissy little fart like you"—he shrugged again—"I ain't so sure about you."

Hahn opened his mouth but Taylor quickly said, "Don't be so quick to answer. Think about it a day or two before you say anything. Both of us's futures could depend on it."

"You'd like me to reject her for something that is not her fault, wouldn't you?" Hahn accused.

"Damn right I would. Now hand me that stick with the bacon on it, will you."

Hahn left the fire without handing Taylor the requested bacon and sought the solitary comfort of his bedroll.

Jessica Taylor

Jess let the stick droop down onto the coals, deliberately allowing the chunk of fat bacon to become crusted with ash and charred wood. She hoped Ederle would break a tooth on something she picked up there.

"Watch it, you dumb bitch. I told you not to let that touch the ashes," Ederle snarled.

"And you watch your language," Jessica snapped back at him, picking the stick up off the coals. "You needn't be crude. There is a child listening, you know."

Ederle grunted. He hunched his shoulders and said nothing further, but it was obvious he was not happy with her.

Jess glanced at the man out of the corners of her eyes, then let the stick droop again. Soon Ederle's supper was once more in contact with the ash.

Loozy looked at her mama and suppressed a giggle, then went back to very carefully tending the pieces of fat bacon that they would share for their evening meal. It was one thing to sabotage the man's food. It would be another to ruin their own.

They had to do the best they could under these trying circumstances. Both of them did.

Chapter 7

"Hold up there a minute," Hahn called.

Taylor looked over his shoulder and frowned at Hahn, who was trailing by twenty feet or so. "What's your problem now?" Taylor demanded.

"I got to get down for a minute. My legs are cramping and my drawers are riding up in my crotch until I just can't stand it."

"Mister, you whine an' snivel more'n just about anybody I ever come across. Well, anybody over two year of age anyhow."

"Are you going to stop? I have to get down and walk. Just for a few minutes."

"You are one useless S.O . . . Never mind. Get down."

Hahn pulled the paint horse to a halt, stood in his left stirrup, and dragged his foot across the rump of the horse. He lowered himself gingerly to the ground, but when he tried to stand his left leg buckled and he sprawled hard onto the ground.

He lost his grip on the rein—or simply forgot to hang on—and the usually steady paint spooked. It snorted and bucked and took off running with the packhorse following owing to Hahn having tied its lead rope to his saddle horn.

Taylor swore, loud and forcefully, and dropped the lead rope of the pack animal that was trailing him. He put the spurs to his brown and sprinted after the fleeing paint. It took him a good ten minutes to run down the paint horse, gather it up, and lead it back to Richard Hahn. By then one of Hahn's reins was broken after being stepped on by the loose animal.

Taylor refused to speak to Hahn, or even to look in his direction, while he stepped down to the ground and rummaged in his saddlebags. He produced an awl and a coil of rawhide, then hunkered down with his back to Hahn and began repairing the broken rein.

The two did not speak again the remainder of the morning.

* * *

"I can't find any tracks," Taylor admitted.

"We're lost?"

"No, of course not. We ain't lost. But their trail is." Taylor sat dispiritedly on the brown horse, hands folded across his saddle horn.

"What do we do now?"

"We look, of course." Taylor hesitated, then said, "I know a, well, a sort of trading post. It's over that way." He nodded his head in a generally southward direction.

"What is a 'sort of' trading post?" Hahn asked.

"It's a hog ranch."

"Fine," Hahn retorted. "So what the hell would a pig farm be doing out this far from anything?"

Taylor gave Hahn a look of disgust and shook his head a little. "You don't know much of anything, do you?"

"I know quite a lot about the things I deal with," Hahn returned, "things about finances and investments that you could not possibly understand. I do not know about cow shit and whatever else it is that you deal in."

Taylor's chin came up and his glare hardened; then he thought about what Hahn said and he let his hackles down. Patiently, as if trying to explain to a half-wit, he said, "A hog ranch is kind of like a trading post that deals mostly in women and whiskey. There's still Indians that wander this country. They don't cause much trouble, so don't get y'self all excited about that. They come to this here hog ranch t' buy whiskey. Which o' course is against the law. Fed'ral law. I dunno if it's against territorial law too, not that it makes no difference.

"Anyway, the place also sells women. Injun women mostly after their husbands trade them for the whiskey. Cowhands, sheepherders, trappers, and the like come here to get laid. The women stay a spell until they figure their debt has been paid off; then one morning they just aren't there no more. Doesn't make much difference because soon enough there will be some other Injun wanting to trade for whiskey. If he has pelts, that's fine. If he don't, then one of his wives will do."

"You seem to know an awful lot about it," Hahn said, his tone of voice as much accusation as comment.

Taylor grinned. "I do. Time was, I was a pretty good customer my own self."

"Jessica thought you were cheating on her, but she never caught you at it in any of the bawdy houses down in Thom's Valley. Now I know where you got your whores."

Taylor backed the brown until he was side by side with Richard Hahn. He gave the man a long look, then without warning backhanded him across the face. Hahn was propelled out of his saddle. He hit the ground hard, his upper lip split and running blood from John Taylor's blow.

"I never," Taylor snapped. "Not never while I was with Jessie, you wife-stealing bastard."

Hahn picked himself up and brushed himself off, then

without comment crawled back up onto the paint horse. He collected his reins and waited silently for Taylor to lead on.

* * *

They reached a stream with a strong flow of water in it and stopped there to water the horses. Taylor knelt beside the brown and cupped the icy-cold water in his hands, let it warm to his touch for a moment, then drank sparingly. Hahn sprawled belly down on the bed of smooth stones that flanked the stream. The smaller man bathed his face, washing away the dried blood left by Taylor's blow; then he too drank.

"We'll be following this creek about a mile, mile and a half upstream from here. Nate built his place at the head of the valley. It's pretty. You'll see," Taylor said, standing and bending backward half a dozen times to loosen muscles drawn tight by hours in the saddle.

Hahn saw and imitated the movement. "Say, this really helps," he exclaimed in surprise.

Taylor gave him a sour look and stepped back onto the brown. He waited without comment and with no discernible expression until Hahn was atop the paint horse; then Taylor nudged the brown's flanks with his spurs and the small party turned up the south-flowing stream.

* * *

Taylor and Hahn skirted a stand of aspen, pale green leaves shimmering on a light puff of breeze. As they squeezed between the nearly white trunks of the trees and the west bank of the stream, there was a loud snort and a stamping of hooves followed by the sounds of a large animal crashing through the thicket.

Hahn jumped and nervously asked, "What the hell was that?"

Taylor grunted. "Nothing much. A cow elk. Had a calf with her. They're spooky anyhow an' all the more when there's a calf with them."

Hahn visibly relaxed. "I've never seen an elk."

Swinging around in his saddle to stare at the smaller man, Taylor said, "You're serious?"

"Of course I'm serious. I have never seen an elk. Not a live one anyway. I've seen pieces of elk brought in by hunters and I've seen those big antlers, but I've never seen a live elk."

"You sure have been sheltered, ain't you?" Taylor observed.

"By your lights I suppose so, but I'm trying to build a good life for Jessica and me. And Loozy too, of course."

Taylor snorted almost as loudly as the elk had done. "You keep forgetting that Jess is still married to me, Hahn. It's one of those little details that seems t' slip your mind. But then I s'pose that decency is just one of those things you haven't got figured out yet, kinda like never seeing a live elk; you don't recognize another man's marriage."

"If Jessie wanted to be with you, Taylor, she would be."

It was not a statement Taylor had an answer for. He faced forward again and concentrated on where they were going.

Ervin Ederle

Erv got off his horse and turned to the blond bitch and her whelp. "Get down now. We gotta walk from here a ways."

The grown-up tossed her head to get strands of falling hair out of her face. The gesture seemed arrogant and cocksure.

Bitch, Erv thought.

"I couldn't possibly walk right now. My limbs are cramping. We need to sit and rest first."

Erv looked toward the west. The sun was on its way down, but it was still a long time before sundown. "We can take a break," he conceded.

They were at the side of a rocky slope that was strewn with loose scree. A barely visible, very narrow path led north along the slope, the path probably worn into the side of the mountain by countless generations of bighorn sheep. He smiled when he saw that nothing seemed to have changed since the last time he was here.

He had found the place by chance that time. He was on the run then with a posse somewhere behind. This treacherous talus slope saved his bacon that time. This time around it would make him rich.

Erv's smile turned into a chortle and he told the woman and kid, "This ain't as bad as it looks. Trust your horse. If the stupid thing wants to bolt and run you over, jump to the uphill side. Let the damn horse pass by over top of you if need be. But remember. The uphill side o' the mountain. That way you won't go sliding down the damn mountain and you shouldn't get hurt too awful bad."

Mother and daughter were both sitting cross-legged on the stones, rubbing their legs—"limbs" the stupid bitch called them and wasn't that a laugh, as if they were too high-mucky-muck to have legs?—and acting like they were the most put-upon creatures on this green earth.

All right, he thought, looking around, not necessarily green. Right here it looked all gray and ugly with a few bits of brown and black tossed in for good measure.

"Come on. On your feet. You've sat on your butts long enough. I want to get to my hidey-hole before too awful long. Or maybe you want to walk across that—" he pointed toward the sheep path—"in the dark."

That got them onto their feet, just as he expected.

"No, you don't, missy. You ain't gonna ride that animal right now. You lead him, just like I said. You!" He pointed at the woman. "You go first. I don't trust neither of you's to follow where I can't turn back and thump you, so you go first an' the kid behind you. You can't get off the path. Not without you fall a couple hundred feet and get all busted up into little pieces. When you come out the other side of this slope, you'll know it right enough. Stop there and I'll tell you where we go next. Go on now. Lead off."

Jessica took a few reluctant, tentative steps out onto the path, her horse following close behind.

"You next," Erv told the kid, who quickly moved to follow her mother.

So far, so good, Erv mused. No one would ever find this place unless he brought them to it. Better yet, they would leave no hoofprints on the rocky sheep path.

He gathered up his reins and followed close behind the butt of the kid's animal.

Chapter 8

Even Taylor, whose way of living took him into the finest country on God's green earth, found this view breathtaking. The waterfall, that was what made it so spectacular. The creek down below was no wider than a man could jump across, but that slim flow of water came pouring down a sheer drop of a hundred fifty feet or more. It splashed onto the rocks below and burst into a soft, shimmering mist before it collected once again into the stream they had been following for the past several miles.

At the head of the narrow valley, close to the pool that lay at the base of the waterfall, the foliage was lush and green, almost tropical in appearance. The dark logs of a cabin were nearly hidden from sight by the naturally watered mix of aspen and pine. The cliff face hanging above the cabin was dotted here and there with small plants that somehow clung to the tiny ledges.

"Damn," Hahn whispered when he caught sight of it.

"Yeah," Taylor agreed. "Damn an' then some."

"I wish Jessie could see this."

Taylor's expression hardened. "Could be that she has."

Hahn immediately sobered and he reached back to touch the butt of the expensive shotgun he was carrying in a saddle scabbard. "That is what we came for, isn't it?" He turned and looked this way and that along the sloping walls of the valley. "You know this man, do you?"

"Aye. I've traded here a time or two."

"Do you think he will tell you the truth?"

"Unless the kidnappers bought him off. Nate, well, he can be bribed. Doesn't have to be with money. He's a funny duck, Nate is. Lives all alone up here 'cept for the Injuns and the folks like me that come by to get drunk or t' get laid. He always has his Injun girls, of course. Keeps them in a sort of a cave dug into the cliff behind his place. Brings them out when somebody wants to have one.

"I dunno who packs alcohol in for him. That's what he uses to make his whiskey. Raw alcohol with . . . with God knows what added to give it flavor an' make it kinda spread out. You would think after all the years I been in this country that I'd know such a thing, but I don't. I suspect Nate worked a deal with some Mexican trader coming up outta Santa Fe or Taos. Prob'ly the same outfit takes away the furs and stuff that the Injuns bring to trade for the whiskey. But that's only speculation. I don't know none of it for certain sure."

"Isn't giving whiskey to Indians against the law?"

Taylor shrugged. "Sure it is, but who in his right mind would pay attention to the fed'ral government?"

"And you think this man might know something about where Jessica and Louise have been taken?"

"I'm sure as hell hoping he does." Taylor leaned out of his saddle, laid one finger against his nose, and loudly blew the other nostril. "One way to find out." He nudged his horse into motion again, leading their little procession toward the cabin at the head of the valley.

* * *

"Shit," Taylor grumbled.

"What's the matter?" Hahn asked.

"Loosen that cinch," Taylor said. "We'll be here long enough that you oughta let those horses blow."

"I asked you a question," Hahn returned. But he did lift his stirrup and begin loosening the cinch on his saddle.

"Don't forget the packhorse."

"I said—"

"I heard you," Taylor snapped. "Reason I cussed was that they ain't here."

"How would you know that?"

Taylor nodded toward the lean-to shelter at the head of the little corral hidden in a copse of pine. "Only horses there are Nate's . . . I seen them before . . . and that one scrawny-ass pinto. That would belong to some Injun, I'd guess. Here to drink an' maybe to trade."

"These Indian, um, girls," Hahn said. "You said you've had one?"

Taylor finished taking care of the cinches on his saddle horse and the pack animal he had been leading. He cocked his head and gave Hahn a sideways glance. "Want t' try one, do you?"

"No, I . . . I'm just curious," Hahn answered, perhaps a little too quickly and too defensively to be credible.

"Look, if you want t' take one for a romp it wouldn't be no big deal. It's not like you're married or anything."

"I said I do not. Excuse me for being curious."

Taylor grinned. "Heard they're wild, did you? Well, believe it. They ain't like white women. Biggest difference is they admit to liking it just the same as a man does. Now, take Jessie—"

"Taylor!" Hahn barked. "Shut your damned mouth. I'll not have you talk about Jessica that way."

John Taylor's grin became even wider. "It's all right, little man. I was just prodding you."

"Well, don't."

"Ain't you done with those cinches yet?"

* * *

The trading post was built to withstand the heavy mountain snows. The logs were thick and the roof slanted at a steep angle. Taylor had to bend to get inside while Richard Hahn ducked his head when he followed the larger man indoors.

"John Taylor. How the hell are you? Haven't seen you in a spell." The man who was speaking had gray hair hanging to his shoulders. He had powerful shoulders and thick arms with muscles corded like rope. He looked like he could whip his weight in grizzly bears, and scars on his arms and his face suggested that he might well have done just that a time or two in the past. "Who's the city fella with you, John?"

"How did he know that?" Hahn quickly said.

Taylor ignored him. "This is the wife-stealing son of a bitch I told you about, Nate."

The trader nodded and asked, "Bring him up here so's you could kill him and bury the body where he wouldn't be found, did you?" He made that sound like an entirely reasonable thing for a man to do.

"No, we're looking for my wife an' daughter, Nate. Somebody has gone and kidnapped the two of them. That's what we came here for. We're wondering, have you seen some riders with a white woman and a girl with them?"

Nate shook his head. "Wish I could help you, John.

You know I sure as hell would if I knew anything, but I don't."

"It was worth asking," Taylor said. "Tell you what, though. Since we're already here, we might as well have a drink before we go. And some jerky. Maybe a bushel. Elk if you got it. If you don't have enough elk, fill the bushel out with mule or moose, but I don't want no damn sheep nor mountain goat."

"Oh, I got plenty elk on hand. Dollar a peck."

"That's all right. The wife stealer is paying. He'll pay for the drinks too."

Hahn gave Taylor a dirty look, but he pulled out his purse and opened it ready to pay.

* * *

"I want to tell you two things," Hahn announced firmly once they were back outside pulling their cinches snug.

"What's them?"

"Firstly, I resent you talking about me that way."

Taylor looked at him and snorted. "Mister, you oughta hear the way I usually talk about you. It'd make your ears turn red an' your balls shrivel up."

"I don't for a moment doubt that," Hahn snapped.

"So what's the second thing?" Taylor pulled his stirrup down and let it dangle ready for use. He reached forward and untied the lead rope from the corral rail.

"The second thing is a question. Why did you buy a bushel of that jerky?"

"Easy. About half the crap you bought back in town will spoil if we're out for very long. Jerky won't." Taylor reached forward and smoothed the brown's forelock and scratched the animal in the hollow under its jaw.

"Do you really think it will take that long to find them?"

Taylor shrugged. "No way I can know that, but what I can tell you is that I don't figure to go back without them. I intend to stay out as long as it takes. All the way down into Mexico or any other damn place. Wherever my wife and little girl are, that's where I'll follow."

Hahn said nothing. He gathered his reins and climbed awkwardly into the saddle of the paint horse while Taylor stepped easily onto the brown.

Jessica Taylor

It was a very good thing the Trent Street Auxiliary could not see her now. None of them would ever speak to her again if they did. She did not need a mirror to know that much.

She had not bathed in two days and had not washed in nearly that long. Her dress was stained with soot from the fire. It had tiny holes burned into it by embers flying up on the night breezes. Holes! In her wonderful dress. The thought made her ill.

And her hair. It must look a sight, all wild and straggly. Much like Loozy's hair did.

Oh, she had tried to keep her precious girl's hair under control, smoothing and combing it as best she could with only her fingers to work with, but it was an impossible task.

"All right. Get up," their tormentor snapped. "You've set around long enough."

"We are tired," Jessica snapped back at him. "We need to rest longer."

"What you need, bitch, is to do what I damn well tell you, that's what you need."

Jessica lifted her chin and glared at the mean, miserable man. "I shall not," she declared.

"Kid, go get on your horse," Ederle commanded.

Loozy looked at her mother and when Jessica did not respond, neither did Loozy.

Ederle bent down with his face close to Loozy's and said again, "Get on your horse. It's time we move."

Louise gave her mother a fearful glance but again refused to respond to the gruff outlaw's commands.

Ederle shifted his attention to Jessica. He stepped over to her, bent down, and said, "Get up. Get on your horse."

Jessica silently defied the order, her chin high and her will steeled, her heart caught high in her throat.

"Suit yourself," Ederle said.

A sense of relief flooded through Jessica. She could defeat this awful man if only she—

The left side of her face suddenly felt on fire and her whole body rocked sideways, immediately followed by every bit as much pain on the right side of her face as the man slapped her—hard—with his whole hand and then backhanded her in the other direction.

Jessica could feel a trickle of blood across her chin and onto her neck.

She screamed. And screamed again the louder when she saw the man take Loozy by the hair and drag her to her feet.

"All right. Please. Whatever you want," she pleaded, scrambling to her feet and tugging at Ederle's arm as she begged him to leave Louise alone. "Don't hurt her. I'll . . . I'll do whatever you say. Please."

Ederle gave her a look of triumph and an appraising stare that she could feel clear through to the bone. It would not do, she realized, to tempt this man into doing more than he intended.

"Please." She took a deep breath and with a foul taste in her mouth because of it added, "Sir."

Ederle snorted. But he released his grip on Loozy's

hair. He motioned toward the horses browsing nearby. "Get on. We'll go now."

"Yes, sir." Jessica beckoned Loozy with her as she hurried to gather up their horses and prepare to leave.

Chapter 9

"They didn't go past Nate's place," Taylor said, disappointment heavy in his voice.

"Right. That's what the man said," Hahn responded.

"Yeah, but you don't understand what that means."

Hahn did not speak but his eyebrows rose in inquiry.

"You see this slope over to the north? That's the best an' easiest way up top. It's the way we generally take cows up and down come the spring an' then the fall. Real easy travel. It's the direction that string o' horses was going the last time we seen actual tracks. I figured to pick them up again right over yonder," he said, pointing. "Now . . ." He shrugged.

"We've lost them?" Hahn asked.

Taylor nodded. "Looks as if we have."

"Then where . . . ?"

"You want an easy answer, I don't have none." His arm swept across the jagged, peak studded horizon. "They're out there, Hahn. Someplace out there."

"What do we do now?"

"Why, we find 'em, of course." Taylor wheeled the brown horse back the way they had just come.

* * *

"Big man! The great tracker. Outdoorsman. Idiot is what I say. You've gone and taken us out of town to no purpose. If we had stayed where we belong, we could have . . . I don't know. Could have identified one of the spies perhaps. Caught him and made him talk. Or reasoned with him. Bribed him. Something! Now we're miles away from where we need to be. We have no idea where the gang is or where they've taken Jessica and Louise. And you, you are no help at all, just running us around in circles to no purpose." Dick Hahn lowered his voice and cursed under his breath.

"Is complaining all you're good for?" Taylor snarled.

"I may complain, but unlike you I get things done," Hahn snapped back at him.

"All right, so tell me. How would you have gone about finding the spy? What would you have done to him if you did find him? If there's an idiot here, Hahn, you're him. Bribe the spy? You think you can buy people. Is that the way you lured Jessie away from home? Did you buy her off with fancy clothes and fancier promises? You get things done? Just what d'you think you've gotten done? Jessie and Loozy are missing, they're in danger, maybe even dead by now, and all you can do is whine. I just wish you'd shut your damn mouth while I try an' work out this trail."

"You haven't done so well at it so far, damn you. And don't you ever say they might be dead. Don't you ever say that."

"Unlike you, Hahn, I'll say whatever is true and I'll say it any time I please. Now if you think you can do better at taking us to them, go ahead and try."

"You know I can't track anyth—"

"Then shut the hell up so's I can pay attention." Taylor bumped the brown forward, anger clouding his concentration. "Shut the hell up," he threw back over his shoulder.

Hahn hurried to catch up.

* * *

"Can't we go a little farther this evening?" Hahn asked.

"No," Taylor said, his tone curt and unfriendly. He unfastened his cinch strap and dragged his saddle off the brown horse, dropped it onto the ground, and went back to pull the pack from the led horse.

Hahn stepped down and stood for a few minutes as if expecting John Taylor to help him unburden his animals, then realized that was not going to happen. Awkwardly and in silence he set about taking care of them himself. By the time he was done, Taylor had a small fire burning, coffee set on it waiting to boil, and a thick chunk of bacon beginning to sizzle.

Dick Hahn chose a spot across the fire from Taylor and sat, the earth hard and uncomfortable beneath him. "God, I hope they're all right."

"Yeah. Me too," Taylor said in a tight, almost inaudible voice.

* * *

Taylor craned his neck, searching the sky from horizon to horizon. He had been doing it off and on since sunrise.

"What is it that you keep looking for up there? If the gang left any tracks, they'd be on the ground," Hahn said. "I may not know much but at least I know that."

"Rain," Taylor told him, bringing his attention back to earth. "I'm looking for rain."

"God forbid," Hahn said. "It's bad enough the way the temperatures are so cold up here in the hills. We don't need rain too."

"Matter o' fact we do need rain. That would soften the ground enough that I might see some proper tracks. As it is the ground's so hard the best I can hope to find is a scrape here an' there, an overturned rock or trampled brush, all the sort o' thing that could be done by an elk or a deer as easy as a horse. Rain might could muss your hair, city boy, an' get your britches wet, but it'd sure help me look for the bastards as has my wife an' little girl."

"My woman, not yours, Taylor."

"Don't push your luck with me, Hahn. You're the one as needs me up here. Only reason you're along with me is the money. You have the money to buy them off with when we find them. But I'm the one as can maybe find them. Don't you be forgetting that."

Hahn turned his face away and pretended to be examining the gravel underfoot.

Ervin Ederle

He was in a very good mood. Things were going well. The woman and her kid were acting right. He smiled to himself thinking how he had put the fear in them. They were pretty thoroughly cowed, all right. And they should be. He meant a good bit of the crap he had told them.

It was just a damned shame he had not brought a bottle along. Or several. After all, it was going to be a couple weeks before he went back down to collect his money. He really should have brought a bottle. Not that he had money to pay for one, and barkeeps tended to watch too close to swipe one. Now, if it was just as easy to steal a bottle as it was to take a horse, well, he would have something to warm his gut in the evenings. On the other hand . . .

He looked across the fire to the woman and the girl, huddled over there about as far away from him as they could get and still receive some warmth from the fire.

Damn woman was starting to look better and better and that was the truth of the matter. She was a bitch but she was a fancy one. He had never had a woman that fancy, nor one that uppity. He wouldn't expect her to be as good as, say, a Mexican trollop or an Injun squaw. But it might be interesting to find out.

Thinking about what the blond bitch would be like twisted his smile into a leer.

He hadn't thought she was paying attention to him, but she was. She saw his expression and read it correctly.

Her face flushed bright red and she quickly dropped her eyes.

"I have to . . . I have to go to . . . to the bathroom," she said.

"Right over there, missy, but you stay in the light, y' hear me? Don't be going past that clump o' brush. Don't go behind it. I got to see."

He would not have thought it possible, but she flushed even darker.

She did not get up or go anywhere.

Apparently, he thought, she did not have to go all that bad.

Chapter 10

Taylor got off the brown and knelt, examining the ground closely for a moment. Then he stood and scuffed at the gravel, stepped back, and looked at the faint mark his boot had made. Finally he turned and looked up at Hahn, who was waiting, still mounted on the paint horse. "I think we may have something here."

"It's them?" Hahn said, his expression brightening and his posture straightening as well. Taylor shook his head. "I don't know as it's them, but I can tell you that it's some-damn-body. Somebody's been through this way."

"Can you tell how long ago?"

"No, I can't. All's I can say for sure is that horses have passed this way not too awful long ago. Could be a day, two days, I really ain't sure." He removed his hat and ran the back of his wrist across his forehead.

"But it's them," Hahn persisted.

"Likely," Taylor conceded. "Nobody would be moving cows up here this time o' year. Everybody running cattle up here already has 'em here and it's too early for them to be brought back down. Shouldn't be anybody up in these hills again for another couple months."

"Could there be a prospector? Someone like that?"

Taylor considered that for a moment, then said, "Could be. I won't guarantee against it, but most prospectin' fellas I've come across don't have more'n one horse. Most often they only go out with a mule or a burro an' no horse at all. From what I see here, there's more than the one animal. An' if you look right here"—he pointed—"you can see that piece of a curve pressed into the soil there where there's a little less gravel. That's for sure a horse hoof. So, no, I don't reckon it's a prospector wandering around up here and it for sure ain't no elk nor deer nor anything like that. Wouldn't be no point to a prospector bein' here since everything has pretty much been looked over anyway. That leaves . . . well, we'll see."

"God, I hope it's them," Hahn said. He pulled his shotgun out of the saddle scabbard and checked the loads.

"Put that thing back," Taylor told him. "We aren't close to whoever this is." His expression was grim, however, when he added, "Yet."

* * *

"Can't we stop for a few minutes? I'm hungry and my backside hurts from all this riding."

"I swear, Hahn, you're more bother than a wagonload of three-year-olds," Taylor snapped.

"I mean it. I need to stop. Besides, I have to, uh, I have to take a leak."

Taylor turned around in his saddle and glared at the man who was the author of all his unhappiness. Or so John Taylor believed anyway. After a moment he sighed. "All right, damn it. Give me a minute to find a good spot."

Fifteen minutes later Taylor reined the brown to a halt beside a trickle of water that sprang out of a nearly vertical hillside. "You can get down now," he told Hahn. "See that spot over there? Build us a fire on those flat rocks an' put a pot of water on to boil. If we're gonna stop here for a bit, we might as well have a swallow or two o' coffee."

"You want me to do it?" Hahn asked.

"Yes, I want you to do it. I'm gonna be busy," Taylor said, stepping down from his horse. He quickly hobbled both his saddle and pack animals, stripped their bridles off, and turned them loose to graze on a patch of emerald-green grass that flourished because of the water.

Taylor started off on foot and Hahn called him back. "Where are you going?"

"Just up there a ways. I want t' see can I find good tracks where we got dirt for a change. It might help me to know what we're dealing with. How many of them. Like that. Get that coffee going. I won't be gone long." He set off on foot, eyes on the ground ahead of him, worry pulling at his features. Jessica. Loozy. Where were they? How were they? What was happening to them now?

He was tempted to hurry. To rush ahead and to find them. But haste was not called for here. Not at all. Thoroughness, that was what was needed.

But oh, it was tempting to hurry.

* * *

"Good Lord, man, where'd you learn to build a fire?"

Hahn looked up at Taylor and scowled. "What business is that of yours, mister?"

"Because I'm the one wantin' to have some noonday coffee, that's what. I been gone a good half hour. By now you shoulda had the fire going an' the coffee all made. Instead you got a pile o' sticks and not even no flame, much less coffee. Lord God, man, you are about useless as tits on a boar hog."

Hahn, bristling, jumped to his feet and thrust his chin out. But he did not take the swing he so obviously wanted to throw. Once was quite enough for that. There was no way he could physically overpower the much larger Taylor.

"Get outta the damn way," Taylor snapped. He stepped forward and brushed Hahn out of the way, then knelt by the haphazard pile of sticks, some of them still green, that Hahn had assembled. Moving with the speed and sureness of long practice, Taylor selected the smallest, driest bits of wood from the pile and reassembled them to his liking. He took a magnifying glass from his pocket, polished it on his sleeve, then focused it on the splintered base of a dry twig to start a small fire. As the tiny blaze took hold and began to strengthen, he added larger and larger pieces until he had a fire the size of a hat.

"Now you can put the water on to start heating. You do have the water ready, don't you?" Taylor waited a moment for an answer but received none. He snorted softly, shook his head, and stood upright. "Never mind, then. I'll get it."

Hahn glared at Taylor for several seconds, then turned and began rummaging in the packs in search of coffee.

* * *

They stopped at the top of a rock-strewn chute that was nearly—but not quite—vertical. It descended for perhaps one hundred fifty feet before reaching the floor of a narrow cut. Taylor stepped down and flipped his stirrup onto the seat of his saddle. He looked back at Hahn and said, "Best tighten your cinch before we start down that thing."

Hahn lifted himself up in his stirrups and peered down at the chute. It looked even taller and steeper than it was. Certainly Hahn found it to be intimidating. "We have to go down that?"

Taylor nodded. "We do."

"Can't we . . . go around? Or something?"

"Nope." Taylor pulled his cinch tight and secured it in place, then mounted the brown, looked back at Hahn, and shrugged. Without another word he started down the chute, shifting his weight far back and allowing the brown horse to pick its way slowly down, a cascade of dust and dislodged rocks leading the way.

Hahn dismounted and began leading the paint horse down. The paint and Hahn's packhorse made it down the chute a good five minutes before he did. Much to Taylor's amusement.

Ervin Ederle

There! The recognition gave him a smug satisfaction. The blond bitch's husband would be too frightened to tell anyone, but even if he did there was no posse on earth that could ferret him out here. He had proven that before. Now Ederle stood on the path . . . goat, sheep, Indian, whatever . . . and peered up at his perfect hidey-hole.

The broad ledge in front of it was perhaps twenty feet above the narrow path. There were no stairs, no ladder or visible handholds, but the climb was not so steep that it could not be easily scrambled, and by a man carrying a pack or bundles of supplies as Erv had also proven the times he had hidden here before.

No one else, no one except the last three members of his gang—or what used to be his gang; with this deal he was retired from all that—knew about this place. No one else ever would.

He looked at the woman and the girl and amended the thought: no one alive, that is.

"Come along. You two can help me carry them bags of stuff up there. Might as well be of some use."

"Carry? Where?" The woman looked confused, not defiant.

Erv grinned, then laughed out loud. "You'll see. Just get down now. You can leave those horses standing. I'll take care o' them later." He would have to lead the horses back down below timberline and turn them loose on hobbles lest they provide a hint of what lay above. Not that he expected anyone to come near, but a man should always be cautious and sensible. That was why Erv had done so well for so long. Cautious and sensible, that was him.

Probably he would need more supplies to keep the females for the two weeks. If he kept them, that is. It might be sensible—certainly it would be easier—to just shoot them and be done with it. He could collect his ransom money and then just fade away with not a soul but him knowing the full truth of it.

The only reason he needed them now was if he had to give a show of good faith. Like if the husband insisted on seeing them before he turned over all that money.

Erv snorted. Good faith! Good faith was for mugs. What Erv cared about was that ransom money. It warmed his heart just speculating about how much it would be. Thousands. How many thousands? Enough to keep him in senoritas for the rest of his days. He was sure it would be that much at the very least.

"Come on now. Take up those pokes from behind your saddles an' carry them. I'll show you the way."

The bags, he noticed, were light. There was not enough food in them to sustain three people for the whole two weeks.

But there was enough for one.

That was something he would have to think about, but first he needed to get some sleep. Watching over the damn females through those several nights getting here just about had him worn down to a frazzle. And before he could sleep now he had to get the woman and the kid settled inside the hidey-hole and take the horses down and . . . there was just an awful lot that still had to be done.

He was just about worn out, that was the truth of

the matter. He could feel it in his chest now. Clutching. Squeezing. Just about worn out, he was afraid.

"Hurry up. We don't got all day."

In spite of Erv's prodding the females were slow to crawl down from their mounts. It took more prodding to get them to carry anything. Lazy bitches. He needed them for the time being but after that, well . . .

He smiled, thinking about the ransom. How much would it be? Thousands? How many thousands? What a delightful question it was to be asking himself, he thought, his smile broadening into a grin.

The woman saw the expression and cringed away, probably thinking he had something else in mind.

Which he did even if not at that exact moment. Funny, the farther they got from town, the better looking the woman became.

Erv yawned and shook his head vigorously back and forth in an attempt to clear the cobwebs from it, then angrily snapped, "Get on up there, damn you. Move!"

It pleased him to see how quickly they scurried.

Two weeks, he thought. Then all that money.

He was smiling again as he grabbed his saddlebags and followed the woman and girl up to the ledge above. Oh, it was going to be such a good life!

Chapter 11

"Over here." Taylor glanced to his right. Hahn was standing behind a screen of scrub oak, pointing at the ground by his feet. He had gotten off his horse in order to take a leak and now seemed to have found something.

"Be right with you," Taylor responded. He reined the brown to the right and stopped behind and to one side from the paint, close but not within kicking range even though the paint horse was not normally a kicker.

Taylor dismounted, wrapped his rein ends in the ragged, tough scrub oak branches, and walked over to stand beside Dick Hahn. "What am I s'posed to be seeing here?"

Hahn pointed again. "Isn't that a hoofprint?"

Taylor looked more closely at the scrape in the red, compacted gravel and said, "Well, I'll be a son of a bitch. 'Tis at that."

Hahn swelled up with pleasure and abruptly nodded his head. "So they went this way," he said, the sentence as much question as statement.

"No doubt about it," Taylor said. "They went this way."

Oddly enough, he received the same sort of pleasure from Dick Hahn's newfound ability to spot a track as he used to feel when then four-year-old Loozy read a new word to him. "That's good," he added. "Real good."

Since he was off his horse anyway, Taylor took a few

extra moments to unbutton his fly and drain his own snake before he climbed back onto the brown.

"No need for that yet," he said when Hahn reached for the butt of his shotgun. "We're still a ways behind them."

"Let me know when we get close," Hahn said.

Taylor nodded. "Count on it."

With Taylor in the lead and the packhorses trailing, they turned off the barely visible path they had been following and scraped past the gnarled and jagged scrub oak in the direction Hahn's tracks suggested.

* * *

"Damn, but this is hard country to track in, and it doesn't help any that there's been somebody's cows using up here lately."

"Using?" Hahn asked.

"Grazing," Taylor said. "Somebody's cows've been grazing up around here."

"If all you can see are a few scrapes on the ground and not an actual hoofprint, how can you tell it was left by a cow and not a horse?"

Taylor looked at him for a moment to see if the question was serious. It was. Hahn was indeed serious about that. Taylor shook his head, marveling at the man's ignorance, then laughed, then pointed off to the left. "Can't you see all the cow flops over there amongst them aspen? A cow is about the only critter on earth that craps like that. Well, cows and buffalo, but there's none o' them up this high. Most o' the animals you find up here leave pellets when they shit. Elk, deer, goats, sheep, they all do. Even the bears kinda do. What we seen along this trail is horse apples." He chuckled. "It ain't always tracks that you look for when you're trailing something, Hahn."

Hahn, chagrined, fiddled with his saddle strings and pretended to adjust something that did not need adjusting. He was not fooling John Taylor.

* * *

Taylor pointed to the ground. "Y'see those horse apples, man? See how shiny they are? Know what that tells you?"

Hahn shook his head.

"It tells you they're fresh. Give 'em a while lying there in the air and that shine will be gone. The apple surfaces will turn dull. Remind me t' show you sometime."

"You don't have to. Really. If there is anything that would fail to capture my interest, horse apples would be high on the list."

Taylor shrugged. "Whatever you say." Then his expression hardened as he thought about Jessica and he said, "About some things, that is."

* * *

Taylor held his hand out to the side, palm toward Dick Hahn. "Stop!"

"What now? Do you see some shiny horse apples glistening in the sun?"

"Don't be a smart-ass," Taylor snapped.

The little string of horses stood looking down into a lush valley with sunlight seeming to sparkle off the emerald-green grasses growing in the middle. It actually was shining on shallow water spreading out from a stream that flowed down the center of the valley.

They were at the edge of a stand of old aspen, some with trunks as big around as a man.

Taylor pointed. "Do you see them?"

Hahn stood in his stirrups and stared but after a moment shook his head and said, "I don't see anything."

"There. Just below them pines. D'you see the gray rocks with a black streak down the left side?"

It took Hahn a while but finally he said, "Yes. I've got that."

"To the right from that and up a ways. There's horsebackers moving through the pines. They're coming onto some quakies now. One, two . . . I see three of them, could be more. I ain't for sure about that." Excitement brought him upright in his stirrups. The horse sensed the change in mood and began to fidget. Taylor dropped his butt onto the saddle and slapped the brown's neck with his rein ends. "Settle down, damn it."

"I think . . . yes, I see them now." Hahn pulled his shotgun from the saddle scabbard. This time Taylor did not tell him to put it away even though they were several miles behind the riders who seemed so close there on the other side of the valley.

Jessica Taylor

Her legs were shaky after all that time on a horse. They trembled so badly she thought she might fall. And yet he kept insisting that they climb this horribly steep path to . . . to God knew what.

Jessica had come to despise that man, so big and gruff and ugly. She turned and whispered to Loozy that he was like one of the trolls that lived under bridges.

Loozy held her hand over her mouth and giggled. Oh, it was good to hear that sound. There was nothing she would not do for her precious child. Nothing. Whatever else happened, Loozy had to survive. Even if Jessica herself did not.

They reached the ledge and saw the opening to a cave. Well, not an actual cave. Even Jessie could see that the dark opening in the face of the mountain was man-made. Shards of broken rock were piled untidily on the flat of the ledge to the other side of the opening, and sticks of burnable wood were piled in a much more orderly fashion on the near side.

"Move right in. Make yourselves to home," the man said. He sounded quite pleased with himself. Almost jovial.

"Are there . . . catamounts or . . . bats or anything?" Jess did not want to speak to the foul creature who held them captive but could not help herself. The cave thing looked so menacing.

"No!" The man snapped the word at her, his mood

suddenly changing from happy to horrid once again. "Now get your asses in there. Put those supplies against the wall beside that box. Fine. Now you two go on to the back. No, don't stop there. All the way back. It ain't far. A few feet is all. You can do it." He scowled. "You better do it."

Jess and Loozy scurried to comply. They pressed against the back wall, back where whatever miner dug this place had given up and gone away.

Walls, floor, and ceiling were all solid stone, uneven where pick and powder had gouged them out of the living mountain. There were two candleholders, sharply pointed bits of iron, that had been driven into the walls, one on either side. At the far back there was a pile of old burlap sacking. Something, coal or foods or something, must have been carried in those.

"Lie down," the man ordered.

Jessica felt a momentary pang of fear for the man's lewd intentions, but it was not that he wanted from them. Not now anyway. She had little hope that this would remain. She had seen the way he looked at her today and there was nothing gentlemanly about it.

"Do it!" he snapped.

"Where?"

"On them croaker sacks, damn it, and be quick about it."

Loozy led the way. She spread the meager few sacks on the hard floor, still littered with chips and tiny shards. She made only one pile and lay on it, placing herself tight against the back wall and motioning for her mother to join her.

Jess, trembling still, lay beside Loozy.

"Roll over. Facedown. And don't dawdle. I'm in no humor to put up with any crap from you." The menace so plain in his voice kept them from wanting to learn what he would do if they displeased him now.

They did as they were ordered.

"Hands behind your backs." His voice was harsh.

Again they complied. Quickly.

"Now hold still. Real still."

The man produced lengths of rope and deftly bound their hands and then their feet, tying them at wrist and ankle.

Then he stood. "Now I know you's bitches can lie with your backs together and untie each other easy as apple pie. Don't! If I come back here an' find either one of you loose, you'll pay for it in blood. You understand me? In blood. Now lie still. I'll be back directly."

He was going to leave them there? Alone? Oh, God in heaven. What if a catamount or a bear or something came along while he was gone? What could they do then? They could not run away or fight back or . . . or anything.

Jess turned her face away so Loozy would not see and began very quietly to cry.

She heard the man's footsteps grating on the bits of rock on the floor and then he was gone, she did not know where.

That should have been a relief. Under the circumstances it was not. What if he just got on his horse and rode away? What if he did not come back? Her tears flowed all the faster at the thought.

"Mama."

"Yes, baby?"

"Don't cry, Mama. We'll be all right."

Jessica wiggled over closer so that she could feel Loozy warm against her. Her baby. Her darling. Loozy had to survive whatever happened here. She had to.

Chapter 12

"No noise now," Taylor cautioned as he brought the brown to a halt and stepped down from the saddle. He took a cotton lead rope from his saddlebags and clipped it to the brown's bit, then tied the rope head high around the trunk of an aspen.

"Should I—"

"Get down," Taylor told him before Hahn could finish his question. While Hahn dismounted, Taylor slid his borrowed shotgun out of the saddle scabbard, broke the action, and checked that two unfired shells were in the breech. He already knew the gun was loaded. The action was mere nervousness. He had never shot a man before, nor wanted to. But for a man who would harm Jessica or his Loozy . . . for that man he would make an exception.

He moved over close to Hahn, who was busy tying the paint. In a soft voice he said, "They're about a quarter mile over there. Settin' up for the night it looks like." While he spoke he untied Hahn's rope from low on an aspen trunk and retied it higher.

"Why—"

"So's the horse don't step over the rope and hurt itself," he answered before Hahn could finish his sentence.

"Oh."

"Anyway, we'll let them settle in while we sneak over there on foot. We go any closer with these horses, theirs will know it an' talk to ours. That would alert them. So we—"

"Talk? What's this shit about horses talking?"

"I don't mean with words, you asshole. I mean they'd whinny or whicker or whatever you might want t' call it. The thing is, they'd make noise. They'd let the kidnappers know something was up. We don't want that."

"No. No, of course not," Hahn said.

"Check your gun before we set out."

"I know how to handle a shotgun, damn it. Better than you, I'm sure." But he checked the gun anyway.

"You got more shells on you?"

Hahn patted his coat pockets, then nodded. "Right here."

"All right, then. Let's go kill us some kidnappers."

* * *

Taylor tugged on Hahn's coat sleeve to stop him and pull him close. He whispered into Hahn's ear, "Damn you, man, you're making too much noise."

"I can't see where I'm going."

"Feel your way with your feet. Jeez, haven't you ever snuck up on anything in the woods before?"

"No, of course not."

"Well, you'd better learn how real quick. If they hear us coming, it could go hard on Jess and Loozy." He let go of Hahn's sleeve and took a deep breath, hoping to calm his nerves. This experience was just as new to him as it was to Dick Hahn.

"Do you think they're in that camp?" Hahn whispered.

"I don't know, but it ain't something I'll take a chance on," Taylor said.

"John, I . . . I want to ask you something."

It struck Taylor that that was probably the first time

Richard Hahn ever called him by his first name. He whispered back, "All right, go ahead."

"Are you scared? I have to tell you, I'm frightened. I'm shaking."

"Sure, but I'm a lot more scared for my girls than I'm scared of the kidnappers," Taylor said. "That's how I think about it anyhow."

"All right, I . . . thanks."

Taylor gave Hahn a pat on the shoulder, almost a friendly one, and they crept on as silently as they could.

* * *

Taylor took Hahn by the coat sleeve and again leaned close to his ear. "I count three of 'em setting by the fire, jawing and drinking coffee. What d'you see?"

Hahn hesitated for a moment, his head bobbing left to right as he counted. Finally he nodded and said, "Yes. Three."

"Here's what we'll do, then. I'll sneak around to the left. You circle right a little way. When I think we've both had time t' get ready, I'll step out of the woods and confront them. We should have plenty of time to get them under the gun. They're all looking into the fire, so their night vision will be gone all to shit. You'll be able to see me plain. Should be so, all right? Just watch for me to clear them trees there." He pointed.

Hahn tried to speak but could not force words out of a fear-constricted throat. All he could do was to nod again.

"Right. Go on now. I'll give you plenty o' time to get ready." Taylor gave Hahn an encouraging push to send him on his way.

Taylor stood for some time, listening to Hahn's progress

through the woods. It was just a damn good thing those three men out there were so busy talking, otherwise they would most certainly have heard Hahn's approach.

The man was not experienced in the woods. But, Lordy, that was hardly an excuse when Jessica's and Louise's lives could be at stake. Surely he could be quieter than that. Hell, a boar hog treading on dry acorn husks wouldn't make that much noise. Taylor could follow Hahn's progress practically every step of the way.

At least, he thought, he would know when the asshole was properly in position. He supposed that might be considered a good thing.

When he thought enough time had elapsed, Taylor moved off to his left, slipping silently through the darkness, feeling his way with each foot before he set it down firmly on the ground.

This was going well, he thought.

Then it was not.

* * *

Dick Hahn was so nervous he was crying. His hands and his lips trembled and he felt sick to his stomach.

Jess. Loozy. He had to save them. He had to be strong. For them.

He took baby steps forward. He was trying to do everything Taylor said he should. He looked across the fire to the opposite side where he expected Taylor to materialize out of the gloom to confront the kidnappers.

It was important for Dick to be there. The kidnappers had to know that they were facing more than just the two shells in John's gun. They had to know that Richard Alton Hahn had come to rescue his lady and her beautiful child.

They had to—

Dick's right foot encountered a . . . something. A root, a rock, perhaps something else. It did not matter. What did matter was that he tripped. He lost his balance and flailed about in an attempt to regain it.

The shotgun suddenly was in his right hand only.

He clung tight to it so as not to drop it and not be able to find it again in the darkness.

His right hand clamped tight into a fist to maintain control over the lovely, custom-made shotgun.

The hammers on the gun were already cocked. It was something he had not wanted to risk forgetting at the last instant.

His right hand closed tight.

On the triggers.

The explosion and fiery blast lit up the woods for a dozen feet in any direction and both charges of heavy buckshot crashed into the tree branches high overhead while Dick felt as if his arm had been broken by the heavy recoil.

Over by the fire the three men leaped to their feet and turned to see.

Dick scrambled with shaky fingers to break the action of the shotgun, extract the spent shells, and fumble fresh ones into the chambers.

Louise Taylor

Loozy was frightened, lying tied hand and foot at the back of some rotten old cave. It was even worse now that she was alone. The man had taken Mama away. He left her hands tied just like Loozy's were but untied her feet and led her outside. That had been . . . she did not really know how long ago. It seemed a very long time.

She could not hear anything and there was nothing to see, nothing but gray rock and the edges of the burlap sacking that she was lying on.

Her nose was running, but she could not reach up to wipe it. She could have turned her head and rubbed her face on the burlap, but that was filthy and smelled sour and she did not want to touch it, much less wipe her face on it.

When she heard footsteps coming into the cave, Loozy tensed and tried to pretend that she was sleeping.

She heard the man's voice. "Lie back down." And she felt Mama lying down close behind her.

She could feel Mama jerking a little. Like she had hiccups. Or like she was sobbing but quietly, trying to keep Loozy from knowing that she was crying.

Thinking about that made Loozy cry again too. But quietly in the hope that Mama would not notice.

When she was sure she had her crying under control, in a soft voice she asked, "Where did you go, Mama? What did he make you do?"

"He just took me outside for a little while."

"But what did you do?"

"It doesn't matter." Mama was crying again. Loozy could hear it in her voice. "It doesn't matter, sweetheart. Try to rest now."

"When will we go home, Mama?"

"When Papa Hahn pays the ransom for us, honey."

"Will it be soon? I want to go home now, Mama." Her tears had dried on her face. She could feel them there. She wanted to wipe her face. Wipe her nose. Scratch the places that itched. She wanted to go home!

"I know, sweetie. I know you do."

She felt Mama take a deep breath.

"So do I."

She felt Mama shift over tight against her back, which was as close to a hug as they could manage lying there on the thin burlap pad with their hands and their feet tied.

"So do I," Mama whispered.

A few minutes later she felt Mama move and then in a cheerful voice say, "Do you know what you should do? You should think of happy things. Think about good things. Think about . . . do you remember when you asked if you could have a kitten? I'll bet you do. I'll bet you remember that. Well, think about the kitten you would like to have. Think about what color it would be and what you would like to name it. Think an entire make-believe kitten."

"Why?" Loozy asked sullenly. "I can't have one. Dick doesn't like cats."

"I will make you a promise, dear. When we get home again you can have your kitten."

"Really? Promise?"

"Pinky swear," Mama said.

Loozy tried to concentrate on a kitten—her kitten, her exact kitten, all soft and furry and purring like Andrea Hemple's cat did when she cuddled and petted it—but it was not easy. Her nose was still running and the burlap smelled just awful and her wrists hurt where the cord was cutting into them and she wanted to go home!

She started to cry again.

Chapter 13

The three men were seated close around their fire, talking and cooking something on dingle sticks held over the coals, scratching and spitting and laughing together. Until Richard Hahn's shotgun fired. Then the man with his back toward John Taylor jumped so hard he fell over backward, fortunately away from the fire or he would have rolled right into it. The two who were slumped round-shouldered with their hats pulled down over their eyes leaped to their feet and threw their hands into the air in surrender.

"Jesus . . . what!"

"Don't shoot. My God, don't shoot."

Taylor dashed forward. Then dropped the muzzle of his shotgun toward the ground. "Lenny. Bob. What the hell are you boys doing out here?"

"John? Is that you?"

Taylor approached the fire, embarrassment writ large on his features. He turned and motioned for Hahn to come out. "It's all right. These are friends of mine."

"We're up here hoping to find an elk," one of the three said.

"Meat hunting? What, the XY can't afford to feed its hands nowadays?" Taylor said.

The tallest of the three shook his head. "We feed good, as you oughta know from all the times you've worked with us. No, elk meat is mighty good an' we won't let any of it go to waste, but what we're really looking for is an extra-fine rack. There's a new fraternal outfit in the valley called the Elk's Lodge. They'd like a really good set of antlers to hang." The man grinned. "Which is what we're doing here. Now what about you?"

Taylor glanced at Hahn before he answered. They were not supposed to say anything about the kidnapping on pain of death. Jessica's and Loozy's death. "This is kind of s'posed to be a secret, fellas. What with a new outfit coming into the valley. We're, uh, looking for fresh graze where a man might run a few head of beeves."

"Not up here, I'd think," one of the hunters said. "You should know that, John. You been in this country long enough to know your way around."

"Yeah, I suppose, but we won't know for certain sure 'til we've looked everything over." He straightened and smiled. "Fellas, let me introduce Dick here. Dick, these no-account wastrels are . . ."

* * *

Taylor pulled a tin cup out of the pack on the horse he was leading. He squatted by the fire and helped himself to a splash of coffee from the battered pot already boiling there. He looked across the fire and grinned. "Randy, I know good an' well you got to have a last name. It's just that I never heard it."

The cowboy known as Randy said, "Smith. I answer to Smith. To a bunch of other names too if you'd rather."

Taylor nodded and raised the cup to his lips, careful to keep them from touching the hot metal. He blew on the steaming coffee and said, "That works for me."

Billy Frake pulled out the makings for a cigarette. He

asked Hahn, "You in the cow business, mister? Forgive me for askin' but you don't look much like a cowboy."

"I'm more in the financing end of things," Hahn said.

"You're a buyer, then?" Tony Francotti said.

"Not exactly," Hahn said with a smile, "but on that order of things."

Francotti nodded as if that explained everything and reached for Billy's makings without bothering to ask. But then the two had worked together for years and were long accustomed to each other's habits.

"What about you, John? Are you working for this gentleman?" Randy Smith asked.

"Oh, you know me, boys. I'm just a day hire."

"You got shotguns, I see. What're you hunting with them up this high?"

Taylor shrugged. "Nothing as handsome as you boys are after. Dick here was thinking we might run into some grouse. Or he might take some rabbits or squirrels for the pot." He grinned. "Thinking of pots, what d'you have in there for supper? We got some beef that has to be et before it goes rotten."

"Beans," Billy said. "We got beans."

"So what say we throw in our slabs of beef to go along with your beans?" He turned to Hahn and said, "How's about you bring out all that good beef? The five of us can eat it before it gets bad."

Hahn started to speak, then thought better of whatever he had been about to say. A protest, Taylor suspected, on account of that beef being very expensive cuts of tender meat. But they really were soon to turn green. Instead of selfishly complaining, Hahn stood and went to his packs to bring out the meat.

* * *

Taylor lay under his soogan staring up at the stars, what of them he could see through the branches of the pines that surrounded them. Someone on the other side of the dying coals was snoring and one of the other boys was smacking his lips. He might or might not have been awake when he did it. The air smelled of wood smoke and pine sap. And something a little more pungent after one of the waddies passed wind, but he was accustomed to that sort of thing. It came with being among men in a rough land.

Hahn had spread his blankets close to Taylor's bed. The man seemed to feel awkward amongst these boys who Taylor knew so well and was so comfortable with. And the truth was, Taylor thought, Hahn was far out of his celluloid collar and necktie way of living. Up here the man was the proverbial babe in the woods.

Oh God. Why did he have to go and think about that? Loozy really was a baby in the woods. Somewhere. Being held somewhere against her will and her mother's.

Where were they now, damn it? How far from this lonely campsite? Were they safe? Had those sons of bitches harmed them?

John Taylor was not a man much given to violence. But if anyone had hurt Jess or Loozy either one . . .

Oh God, he thought. He moaned aloud and rolled over, but there was no comfort to be found.

Jessica Taylor

Jess tried to muffle the sounds of her sobbing and the tremors of her shaking. She did not want to frighten Loozy even more than the child already was. Certainly she would never tell Loozy what that awful man had done to her out there, but she could not help crying and wishing for . . . for what?

For rescue? No one could possibly find them out here so far from civilization.

For ransom? Dick and she did not have the kind of money the man was demanding and he would not break the trust of the bank to obtain it. That, she feared, was not so much a matter of integrity as that he would not risk a prison term for having stolen the investment funds.

Jessica surprised herself with that thought. Did she have so little confidence in Dick as to think he would put his own welfare above that of herself and Louise?

The truth was that she was not sure. That in itself was something of an indictment.

And no one else knew they were up here. There was no one else to bring them succor.

The man told her what he had written in his note to Dick. Told her and then laughed at his own cleverness, for there was no gang. No one watched down there in Thom's Valley. No one knew other than the man and Dick.

Jessica trembled. And nearly jumped out of her skin when the man came to the back of the adit—that was what the man called it, not a tunnel but an adit—and lay down beside her.

She thought the son of a bitch was going to attack her again, right there beside Loozy where the child could hear and even feel the terrible things he did to her, but all he did in fact was to lie down and press himself tight against her spoonlike so she was sandwiched between Loozy and him.

It was bad enough that he put his arm over her and slid his hand inside her bodice so he could fondle her, his hand painfully rough on tender flesh, but the other would have been worse.

Mercifully soon he began to snore, the noise of it close behind her ear.

Jess squeezed her eyes tight shut and tried to will herself into the peaceful freedom of sleep, but that release would not come to her.

Chapter 14

Tony Francotti apologetically said, "I'm real sorry, John, but we don't have anything to spare. We brought just enough for five days and we been out four already."

"That's all right. We understand." Taylor reached for the coffeepot and helped himself to a swallow or two.

"If we had extra we'd sure give it to you, though."

"I know that, Tony. Don't give it a thought." He smiled and raised his cup to blow on the dark brew it held.

"You boys are running short, are you?" Randy Smith asked.

"Ayuh. A little bit." The truth was that Dick Hahn hadn't known road apples from apple pie when it came to laying in supplies for a trek into the mountains. Most of the things he had bought, like the fresh beef, was already going bad and would have to be thrown away. The ready-made biscuits were reduced to crumbs. Taylor did not want to embarrass the man by saying so, though. They had the jerky he had bought at Nate's hog ranch back by the waterfall but not much else.

"You could go down to Embry's store," Billy Frake suggested.

"Embry's?" Taylor asked, his eyebrows rising. "Don't reckon I know it."

"It's in the next drainage over," Billy said, waving vaguely toward the southwest.

"Closer than Nate Dollar's place?" Taylor asked.

"I'd say so, yes, and with lots more to choose from. Plenty cheaper too," Billy told them.

Taylor grunted. "Reckon this Embry fella has bacon? I got me a hankering for some bacon."

Tony laughed. "Bacon and beans, that's what a cowhand lives on."

"Ain't that the truth?" Billy said. "As for Embry's, he's for sure got bacon. I've never bought of it to judge the quality, but I've seen slabs of cured bacon hanging in the rafters, so I know it's there."

"Maybe we'll drift over that way. Wouldn't hurt to talk to this Embry anyhow. Ask if maybe he's seen anything of my women."

Hahn gave him a dirty look, which Taylor ignored.

"Women?" Randy asked, his head coming up and keen interest showing in his expression. "What women?"

"I, uh, guess maybe we forgot t' mention that last night. We, um, we're looking for some sons of bitches that kidnapped my wife an' daughter. They're holding 'em for a ransom." He inclined his head toward Hahn. "Which Dick here is gonna arrange to pay."

"You carrying a bunch o' ransom money, are you?" Smith asked.

Taylor did not know Randy-who-called-himself-Smith all that well and certainly was not going to trust the man with the idea that he and Hahn might be easy pickings . . . just in case he was inclined toward such things. "Hell no," he said with a grunt and a turn of his head to spit. "I said Dick will arrange to pay, not that we're carrying a peck of gold with us. No, first we have to settle on a price and then see their bona fides, maybe bring my daughter back with us while we go back to town to fetch the money an' meet them someplace close in."

"Damn, John, that's lousy. I sure as hell wish you luck with it," Billy said.

"Me too, John. You can count on that," Tony added. "If there's anything we can do . . ." Tony's voice trailed away and he became silent, looking faintly embarrassed at his own lack of usefulness in this situation.

"Yeah, sure," Smith said although with considerably less conviction than was in the voices of his companions.

"Tell us again how to get over to this Embry's post," Taylor said.

* * *

Embry's store was a full day's ride, which put it nearby by high country standards. It was not as handsome as Nate's had been, but it was a great deal larger. It lay at the mouth of a deep, narrow valley that had water but little wood.

"Why would anyone build in such a remote place?" Hahn asked as they descended a winding path down the north slope of the valley.

Taylor swiveled around in his saddle. "Could be he started out trading with Injuns and wanted to be out amongst 'em." He grinned. "Could be he just hates folks and doesn't want t' see too many of 'em all to once."

"That certainly clears things up," Hahn responded.

"Always willing to help," Taylor laughed. He turned forward in his seat again but left the reins slack so the brown could pick its way down without interference from him, it not being a good idea to disrupt the footing or the balance of a horse on a mountain trail.

The downhill side of this trail fell off at a less than precipitous angle, but even so it would be no easy ride to tumble off it. Hahn, Taylor noticed, kept urging his paint close to the uphill side of the path. The paint was neither as steady nor as surefooted as the brown horse and it was not a good idea to interfere.

Not that it was John Taylor's responsibility to look out for Dick Hahn. If the man wanted to ride his horse off the side of a cliff, he was welcome to do so as far as Taylor was concerned.

"We'll be there in half an hour or so," Taylor called back to the man.

* * *

"Pull the packs and set 'em over there," Taylor instructed. "It's late, so we'll stay the night here."

Hahn bristled. "Who the hell appointed you the boss?"

"All right, do what you damn please, but I'm staying here tonight. I intend to have a drink or two and get a good night's sleep. I couldn't sleep worth a shit last night."

Dick Hahn scowled but he unloaded the packhorse as well as unsaddling the paint. Both animals, along with Taylor's, were turned into the spacious corral adjacent to the sprawling store. There was water from the nearby creek diverted through a trough inside the corral, and the hay bunk was nearly full.

Three horses and a mule were already standing head down and hipshot inside the enclosure. Their interest perked up with the arrivals of the newcomers. One large gray snorted and pinned its ears flat.

"Aren't you worried they might fight?" Hahn asked.

"They'll work out amongst themselves who is gonna be in charge," Taylor said. "Now come on. Let's go see what this Embry fellow has in the way of food and liquor." He set off for the front of the store with Dick Hahn at his heels hurrying to keep up. Taylor, and therefore Hahn behind him, ignored the squealing and stamping of the horses left in the corral.

Ervin Ederle

Ah, now. Dark and dusky Mexican maidens. Two of them, naked as peeled eggs, their breasts like pointy little pears, smooth and firm and lovely. Bending over him to offer fruits and cervaza . . . and themselves. Oh yes.

Damn! Erv's eyes snapped open and the dream vanished. Not a bad dream, though, and one he intended to make come true in very short order.

He sat up and looked at the sleeping woman and her kid. They represented cash. They represented his future. They were what would allow him to make that dream happen.

He still was unsure what he would do with them once her man paid up. The sensible thing would be to just kill them and be done with it. If he was caught he would hang for the kidnapping. If he killed them, well, the sons of bitches could not hang him more than once. And anyway he was not going to be caught. He was an old he-wolf of the hills and he knew how to get along. Especially without the deadweight of a woman and a kid dragging him down.

On the other hand, there are times when a man needs a woman, and this woman, fancy though she might be, should be good enough for that.

Erv yawned, stretched, shifted over onto one cheek, and loudly passed wind.

He stood and took a drink from the water bag—damn shame he did not have any whiskey, which was what he really wanted—and swished it around in his mouth for a moment to clear the foul taste of sleep before he swallowed.

He stretched again and grimly smiled to himself. Yes, sir, a man does want a woman at times and in the mornings most of all.

He stepped closer to the woman, curled on her side with the kid small in the bend of the woman's body. He reached out one foot and nudged the woman with the toe of his boot. More or less inserted it in the crack of her butt. She came awake with a start and rolled onto her back. He bent down and untied the loop of cord that had been around her ankles.

"What . . . ?"

"Get up," Erv ordered, enjoying the power he had over her.

"Why? What?"

"You know what an' you know why. Now get up and come outside."

"Please no." Her hair was disheveled and there was a smudge on her left cheek, but she was still a handsome filly for all that.

Looking at her, knowing that she would do as he said, whatever he said, made his desire swell all the more.

Erv chuckled and said, "It makes no never mind to me, missus. If you want t' lie there beside the kid an' do it where she can get some education on the subject, well, that'd be just fine by me."

The woman came quickly to her feet. She refused to look at him. But she would do what he told her to do. Whatever he told her to do.

"Outside," he said.

Later, his immediate urges satisfied, he snorted and said, "I'm gonna untie you and your kid. You can cook yourself something to eat. Whatever you can find there. Me, I'm gonna be gone for a day or two. Gonna go get us some supplies. If you want to run away you should ought to know that I'm taking all the horses. You'd be afoot and these mountains still hold hostile Indians as well as the wild stuff. Bears and mountain lions and coyotes and like that. So I wouldn't run was I you." He laughed, the sound as much derisive snort as it was laughter. "But you do what you want, y'hear? Just don't hold me responsible do you get yourselfs killed up here."

Ederle took up his canteen—the females could drink the snowmelt coming down the mountainside if they got thirsty—and catch rope. He took a last look around, then left the woman standing outside the mouth of the adit while he walked back down to the game trail and disappeared down the mountain and into the trees below.

Chapter 15

Phil Embry would measure larger around his middle than he did from floor to scalp. He had a round, smiling face and a thick, black beard but only a few meager fringes of dark hair rimming his head.

"Welcome, gentlemen. What can I do for you this lovely day?"

Taylor smiled back at him. "You always this friendly?"

"But of course. Have you come here to shop or, um, something else?"

"First off, Mr. Embry—"

"Phil. My name is Phil. Please call me that." He practically beamed with pleasure.

"Yes, sir, of course," Taylor told the man, "First off, do you have something to drink?"

"I have sarsaparilla." Embry's grin was sly. "Or perhaps you were wanting something a mite, shall we say, stronger."

"Right now I'd down a shot of mule piss if there was alcohol in it," Taylor said.

"He would too," Hahn put in from two paces behind. Taylor gave him a dirty look. Meanwhile Embry was busy setting out tin cups and a pottery jug.

"Fifty cents for a cup or five dollars for the whole thing," the proprietor said.

"That seems kind of high," Taylor said. He was accustomed to ten-cent drinks, fifteen at the most.

"Very," Hahn agreed, moving up beside Taylor.

Embry nodded. "You gentlemen are welcome to go elsewhere for your refreshments if you prefer."

Taylor laughed. "An' how far is it to the next town?"

"Forty miles or thereabouts. Maybe a little more."

Taylor turned to Hahn and said, "Pay the man five dollars." He picked up the jug and both cups and carried them outside, Hahn again following. But not until he handed Phil Embry a five-dollar half eagle.

* * *

"You're drunk," Hahn said, his voice slurred.

Taylor considered the accusation for what seemed a long time, then leaned forward and said, "Y'know, you are right 'bout that." Then he laughed, the sound much like a giggle except that grown men do not giggle. Ever. He thought about that and giggled again. That is, he laughed again.

The two were seated cross-legged on the ground, leaning back against the lowest rail on the corral fence. They had the jug placed between them and both cradled their tin mugs with care lest they spill any of Phil Embry's popskull. The liquor had been on the edge of being undrinkable to begin with but was tasting better and better as the level in the jug diminished.

"You hungry?" Hahn asked.

"I could stand something t' eat," Taylor said.

"Then let's go get something to eat."

"Good idea." Taylor stood with some difficulty, having to grip the fence rails and use them to help pull himself upright. He was not steady on his feet, but he did manage to get upright.

Hahn was not so fortunate. He tried to stand, failed, tried again. And failed again.

"Now who's drunk?" Taylor taunted.

"You are."

"Yeah, but you are too, you asshole."

"Stop calling me that and help me get up, damn it," Hahn said, waving one hand feebly.

Taylor leaned down, almost overbalanced, and grabbed hold of the fence to keep himself from falling. With his other hand he clutched the back of Hahn's coat collar and hauled the smaller man to his feet.

"Don't forget the whiskey," Hahn said.

"Right. Can't forget the whiskey." Taylor retrieved the crockery jug and in the fading daylight the two headed rather unsteadily toward Embry's store.

* * *

Taylor finished his bowl of red beans and rice, belched hugely, and stood up. He felt almost sober after his meal. Hahn was still eating. Taylor walked over to the counter where Phil Embry was talking to a customer.

"Gentlemen," he said, nodding.

Both men turned to look at him.

"I hope you don't mind if I interrupt here," Taylor said.

"No, we're just jawing," Embry said. "Is there something you need?"

"There surely is. I'm hoping you can give me and the little fella over there some help."

"That depends on what you're wanting. Can maybe I sell you some horses? This gentleman here just swapped me a pair of saddle horses complete with their riggings. I could give them to you cheap," Embry said.

The large gentleman in question—he was as tall as Taylor but thicker in the body and much older—leaned an elbow on Embry's counter and looked bored.

"I'm looking for information," Taylor said.

"About . . . ?"

"A woman and a little girl," Taylor told him.

"Little girl? I don't traffic in them, friend. Women I have but a little girl? Um, I might know of a man who could help you with that but . . ."

"No, no, you got me wrong. I'm not looking for what you think. It's just that my wife and daughter have been . . ." He hesitated, then decided to go ahead. "They been kidnapped. I'm trying to find them. Trying to get them back."

The customer swiveled his head first toward Hahn and then toward Taylor. He stood upright and looked from one to the other again. "Your wife, you say?"

"That's right. They was taken a couple days ago and we're trying to find the gang that took them."

"A gang, you say?"

"Yes, sir, that's what the ransom note said."

"Do you got a posse with you?"

"No," Taylor said. "The note warned against telling anybody. I . . . maybe I shouldn't be telling this to you but . . . we got to find them. Got to. An' how're we gonna know if anybody's seen them if we don't ask? Tell me that much." He shook his head, saddened and still more than a little drunk.

"So there's just the two of you going against a whole gang of kidnappers?" the big fellow asked.

Taylor decided perhaps he should not be quite so open about his and Dick Hahn's intentions. He shook his head and said, "Not going up against. We couldn't expect to fight a whole gang of men. We're just trying to find them to . . . what you might call 'arrange' to get them back."

"How can we help?" Embry asked. He sounded like he meant it.

"I'm just asking have you seen a bunch of men traveling with a woman and a little girl? Yellow hair, the both of them. And scared. They'd both be scared, I know that for certain sure. Have you seen anything of them?"

"Not me," Embry said. He looked at his customer and said, "What about you, Erv? You see any such crowd?"

"Sorry," Erv Ederle said with a shake of his head. He gave John Taylor a sad smile. "Wish I could help you."

Ervin Ederle

Erv stepped down from his saddle and looked around. There were a handful of horses, most of them pretty scruffy, standing hipshot in the corral. Not enough of them to suggest a posse might be inside Embry's place. That was the only thing he was worried about. And that only mildly. There was nothing about him that would connect him with the kidnapping even if there was a baker's dozen of lawmen inside there.

He unsaddled all three of his horses and hung the saddles on fence rails, then turned the horses in so they could get to hay and water. After they were taken care of he went inside, his saliva running in anticipation of Phil's whiskey. If there was one thing Phil Embry did well, it was to mix up a fine whiskey out of raw alcohol and . . . something. Phil never let on what it was he used to make his drinks. Probably that was just as well. There are some things a man might not want to know.

Once inside he tipped his hat back and ambled over to the counter where Phil was doing something or other out of sight beneath the planks.

Phil greeted him with a smile. "Hello, Erv."

"Hello your own self, Phil. How you been?" Ederle reached into a large apothecary jar on the counter and fetched out a peppermint stick. He pushed the whole thing into his mouth and crunched the confection between his teeth.

"Middling. What can I do for you, Erv?"

Erv looked around. There was an Indian poking around the stacks of goods for sale and over on one side there were a pair of men hunched over bowls of food. The big one looked mildly familiar. He could not get a good look at the smaller of the two. Phil did not seem worried, so neither did Erv. He was confident that Embry would have tipped him off if the strangers were law dogs.

"The thing is, Phil, I'm broke. I got fourteen cents in my kick and I need some eatables. I got something going up in the high country and I need food to carry me through."

"I don't give credit. You know that, Erv." He smiled and added, "And you can pay me a penny now for that candy you just ate." The smile was there, but there was no doubt that he meant it too. Ederle reached into his poke and paid Phil his penny.

"Thanks." Embry dropped the penny into a metal box beneath the counter. "Now then, what were you saying?"

"I'm not asking for credit, Phil. I got trading material. I got two good horses complete with their riggings that I can swap you for the supplies I need."

"These horses, do you happen to have bills of sale for them?"

Erv grinned and shook his head. "Not exactly. But I could make one up if you got pen and paper." His grin got wider. "Anyway, these should be entirely safe so long as you sell them south." He laughed. "You might have a problem was you to take them up to, say, Thom's Valley."

"I don't have any customers from there," Phil said, "not as a regular sort of thing."

"Then we can do a little business?" Erv asked. He needed those supplies. If, that is, he kept the woman and the kid in case the husband needed some bona fides. If Phil would not make the trade, he would just have to kill the both of them and hope the husband would not balk when it came time to pay up.

"You know me, Erv. You know we can work a deal. Would you like a drink?" As if there was any question about that.

* * *

Erv was hunched over his whiskey—it was as good as he remembered—when the big fellow from the table came over. The little one turned and Erv got a look at him. Damned if it wasn't the banker whose wife and kid he had stashed up in that old adit.

Except . . . the big man got to saying how the woman was his wife that was kidnapped. Which made no sense. Erv had watched her. Watched her come and go. Watched the husband too. Or who he thought was her husband except now this man was saying she was his.

Surely he hadn't snatched the wrong woman. Had he?

So anyway, these two were out hunting for her and the kid. Not that there was a chance in hell of them finding them. Not where Erv had put the two of them.

And what did he care whose woman she really was? Just so long as they paid the ransom. That was the important thing. The only important thing.

Once he worked that out, Erv felt better about the situation. Just so long as these two paid him his ransom. Which he would arrange back in Thom's Valley in a couple weeks from now. Somehow. He hadn't quite worked out the details yet when it came to collecting his money. But he would. He surely would.

"Phil, give these gentlemen drinks, would you? Put them on my account."

The big one was standing right square beside him. The fellow looked at him and said, "Thank you, mister. That's mighty kind o' you."

"My pleasure," Erv said. And he did mean that sincerely. He was smiling when he raised his cup for another swallow of Phil's good liquor. Yes, sir, the cat did get the canary.

Chapter 16

Taylor woke with a splitting headache and cotton mouth. Rather foul-tasting cotton at that. Like it had been pulled out of the sludge in Grandma's outhouse before being stuffed into his mouth.

He sat up on the side of the bunk in Phil Embry's back room, winced at the intrusion of light, and managed to look around. Hahn was snoring two bunks down. They were alone in the room although he seemed to remember there being someone else there the previous evening. Or morning. It had been past being merely late by the time they gave up the drinking and sought their blankets.

The blowout last night, Taylor knew, was simply a reaction to the tensions of looking for a bunch of kidnappers. And, much more, the fear both men felt for Jessica and Louise.

Both men, Taylor conceded. Dick Hahn genuinely cared for his wife and daughter. That thought was repugnant but inescapable. Whatever John Taylor might think of the little man, he did really care about Jess and Loozy.

He stood, yawning, and shuffled over to the bunk where Hahn was still sound asleep.

Reaching down, he nudged Hahn in the ribs and received a snort in return, so Taylor nudged him again. That did little, so the next step was to shake him. Taylor was considering finding some water to splash on his face when Hahn finally opened his eyes.

"Leave me be," he grumbled.

"If you want but I'm going after them."

"So what else is new?"

"You don't remember?"

"What I remember is that I want to sleep some more," Hahn complained.

"Go ahead an' sleep if you want, but I'm gonna follow up on what that fella told us last night."

"Fellow? What the hell fellow are you talking about now?"

"The big guy who bought us drinks. Don't you remember him?"

"Yes. Sort of. What does he have to do with anything?"

"He said he saw a bunch that might be the men we're looking for. Six men, he said, an' two women. He said they were bundled up and he took them to be Indian squaws, but there were the two of them along with a hard-looking group of men."

Hahn shot upright on the side of his bunk. "Why didn't you say so? Damn, man, it's well past daybreak. What are we doing here now?" He grabbed his shirt and headed for the outhouse.

* * *

"Shit!"

Taylor looked up. Hahn did not normally use language like that.

"Some bastard has stolen my purse."

"All of it?"

"Everything I had in that little purse. That isn't all I have with me, thank goodness." Hahn reached inside the crotch of his drawers and pulled out another soft leather purse fastened closed at the neck with a drawstring. He grinned. "Something only Jessica would find."

Taylor quickly looked down and fussed with the boot he was in the process of putting on.

"I . . . I'm sorry," Hahn quickly said. "I didn't mean . . ."

"Yeah, sure," Taylor said, still without looking at the man again. "Are you ready? We still have to get those eatables we came after."

Hahn said nothing but followed Taylor out into the store where Embry was perched on a stool watching an Indian woman and a boy of eight or nine who were examining the merchandise.

Dick Hahn approached the counter, still stuffing his shirttail into his trousers. "That man who was here last night. The big fellow. Do you know him?" he asked.

Embry nodded.

"I think he stole my purse."

The storekeeper threw his head back and laughed. Once he finally got over his fit of chuckles he shook his head, wiped his eyes, and said, "That sounds like Erv all right."

"What?"

Embry chuckled a little more. "Erv is a thief, no doubt about it. Goodhearted fellow but the man is a thief."

"You could have warned us," Hahn snapped.

Embry's amusement vanished as if it had never been. He stared at Hahn for a moment, then said, "If you aren't man enough to see to your own self, I'd be wanting nothing to do with you. Now . . . you got business here? State it. If not, clear out. You've overstayed your welcome."

Taylor took Hahn by the elbow and pulled him away. "Go check on our horses. Make sure they haven't 'strayed' along with that fellow."

Hahn sent decidedly sour looks first toward John Taylor

and then toward Phil Embry. But he did leave, slamming the door on his way outside.

Taylor looked at Embry and shrugged. "Sorry 'bout that."

"The little fella doesn't get out much, does he?"

Taylor grinned and said, "We could use some stuff."

"If I have it. What's more, if it's you doing the buying I won't even raise the prices on you."

"Thank you, sir. Now I figure we'll be needing a half bushel of spotted beans. Couple slabs of bacon. Quart of molasses. Two of coffee, ready ground if you've got it. And say . . . are those leather britches I see in that basket?"

"You mean those dried string beans? Yes, sir, they are."

"Better let me have a peck o' them too. Oh, and candles. How about lucifers? You got any of those sulfur-tipped matches?"

"Sure."

"Some of those too, then. Two, make it three boxes. And paraffin. I'll want to coat the boxes o' matches so they don't get wet and go bad."

"Anything else?"

"Probably but I won't think of the rest of it until we're half a day gone."

"That's the way I always am about such things," Embry agreed. "Always come up with my best arguments too after the lamp is blown out and everybody gone home."

"That's called human nature," Taylor said. "Anyway, get that stuff together, would you, please. I'll go outside and check on my . . ." He stopped there, not quite knowing how he should refer to Dick Hahn. The wife-stealing son of a bitch was damn sure not his friend. Companion, he supposed would cover it. Companion, then. "I'll be right back."

* * *

Taylor's head was splitting and he was sure Hahn's would be too, but that did not stop the little man. Hahn hurried out to the corral and started saddling. He was done almost as quickly as Taylor finished their shopping, collected money from Hahn to pay for it, carried it outside and loaded it into the packs, and saw to his own horse. And as soon as he was done he went out of the gate and sat on top of the paint horse impatiently drumming his fingertips on the rawhide covering on his saddle horn well while Taylor rode the brown's morning jumps out of the animal and could join him.

"Are you finally ready?" Hahn demanded.

"Waiting on you," Taylor shot back at him. Lord, he should know better than to drink that much.

Jessica Taylor

"Put that wood on the fire." Jessica sighed. "This won't last long, so I'll go down and break up some of the fallen wood. I saw some below the path. It should be dry enough."

"Don't be gone long, Mama." Loozy sounded frightened. But then she had every reason to be. Jess was scared half to death herself, almost as much since the man left as when he was there. She half hoped something would happen to him and he would never come back, half hoped that he would return because she and Loozy were lost up here. They would never find their way back home on their own. Or live long enough out here in the mountains even if they knew where they were going. But she did not dare show any of her fear to her daughter. Not if she could help it anyway. Jess sighed again and took a deep breath.

She stooped and kissed Loozy on the forehead. "I won't be long, baby."

It was barely daylight and already Jessica's eyes burned with fatigue. She had spent much of the night fearfully waiting for the man to return. It had been late, probably close to morning, when she finally fell asleep. She was fairly sure Louise had had the same difficulty.

"Have you seen an ax or anything like that, baby?"

"There's a saw over there." Loozy pointed toward a dusty keg, behind which was the handle portion of a rusted Swedish bow saw. However rusted, it would do.

Jessica pulled it out from behind the keg and took it with her outside into the chilly morning air. She stretched and looked toward the east. On any other morning, she realized, this would have seemed an absolutely glorious daybreak with the yellows and golds and purples streaking the sky. She shivered and picked her way down to the path they had come up and then farther down the rock-strewn slope.

She reached a tangle of what John probably would have called a blowdown. She remembered something similar when he had taken her on a ride once. They rented horses and took a picnic basket and rode into the foothills. He took her to a little babbling stream and laid out the picnic there and they ... Jessica blushed when she thought about that day with John. She shook off the memory, pushed a stray wisp of hair behind her ear, and set about industriously sawing at the deadwood of the blowdown.

When she had what she thought should be enough for a breakfast fire, she gathered up the fruits of her labors and climbed back up to the adit.

"Why haven't you gotten the fire going, Loozy? There's enough wood to get it started."

"What am I supposed to start it with, Mama? It went out during the night."

"Coals, sweetie. There should be some coals in the ashes."

"I thought about that but there aren't any. They're all dead."

"Damn," Jessica mumbled. She set her armload of dry wood down beside the cold stone wall of their prison and prised a sliver off a piece of wood, then used it to stir around in the ashes looking for coals. She found nothing. "Do you see any matches, sweetie?"

"No. I did find a piece of something I think is flint."

"What about steel?"

"There's plenty of steel in here," Loozy said. "We could use . . . I don't know . . . the blade of that saw maybe. But we don't have any tinder. You need tinder to start a fire with flint and steel, don't you? I've seen Daddy start fires and he always used some sort of tinder."

Jess slumped down onto the sharp rock shards that littered the floor. She put her face in her hands and willed herself not to cry. It would all be fine. Just as soon as Dick paid the ransom, it would be fine. She told herself that over and over again until she almost believed it.

"Come along, sweetie. If we can't cook we can at least wash. We have water, after all. And I think . . . I think there is a little rice in that bag. We can't eat it raw, but if we soak it maybe we could eat it. In the meantime we can chew a little of this jerky." She tried her best to fashion a smile.

Jessica held Loozy tight, rocking back and forth very slightly. "We're going to be all right, sweetheart." Perhaps if she said that often enough, she thought, she would begin to believe it.

Chapter 17

Taylor drew rein at the head of a narrow valley. Hahn nudged his pinto up beside Taylor and asked, "Where do we go now?"

John Taylor shook his head. "Damned if I can see a way up from here." He snorted in disgust and dismounted, Dick Hahn quickly following.

Ahead of them the incline to the next rise was too steep for a horse, although a man on foot would have little trouble scaling the rocks and scattered brush.

"This is the way that thief told you to go? Are you sure?"

"For the tenth time," Taylor said, exasperated and becoming angry, "yes, I'm sure this is the way the guy said."

"You don't have to snap my head off about it," Hahn returned. "I'm not the one who said it."

Taylor kicked the gravel underfoot and said, "Hold these horses, will you? I want t' see can I find tracks of any sort. See if maybe horses have been through here. Though I doubt it. I don't see how they could." He handed the reins of the brown to Dick Hahn and tied the end of the packhorse's lead rope to his saddle horn.

Hahn let the four animals, the two saddle mounts and both packhorses, drop their heads and pick at the meager foliage the valley offered. After a few minutes he walked them back down toward the open foot of the canyon that had led them here, to where there was a heavier growth of grass stems. The patient animals began to graze while Hahn fidgeted.

After fifteen or twenty minutes Taylor returned. He did not look happy. "I climbed halfway up there. Found some tracks to be sure, but they wasn't horses. Mule deer and some mountain sheep but no horses. A couple places I had trouble making it up on foot. There's no damn way a horse could climb it."

"Why would that man lie to us?" Hahn grumbled. "The son of a bitch is a thief. Now we know he's a liar too."

"I dunno," Taylor said. "Maybe he wanted to lull us away from our worries so's we'd sleep easier an' let him rob us. Could be as simple as that. Or maybe we'll never know what reason he had. If he had any reason at all. Some folks just plain enjoy being ornery. He could be one of that sort." He bent down, plucked a grass stem, and began chewing on the end of it. The hint of juice in the stem tasted faintly sweet.

"I can tell you this," Hahn said with conviction. "If we ever see the bastard again I'm going to walk right up to him and punch him in the face. I might not be able to whip him, but I'll get at least one good lick in."

Taylor peered down at the little man and mused, "By Godfrey, Hahn, I believe you mean that. You might not have much in the way of brawn, but you didn't get left out when guts was passed around."

"Why, thank you, John. Thank you very much for saying that."

"It's just the simple truth." Taylor reached for the reins of his brown. "Come on, damn it. We need to retrace where we been and see can we pick up the trail again."

* * *

"Hold up a minute." Taylor stopped his horse and stepped down from the saddle.

"Is something wrong?" Hahn asked.

"Two things," Taylor said. "First, I gotta take a leak." He grinned. "Put some water into this dry valley. Second, I'm getting hungry. Might as well take advantage of the shade while we got some." He pointed to a stand of runty cedars.

Hahn nodded and climbed stiffly down from his mount. "I don't know how you stand all the riding you do. It has my knees so wobbly I'm half afraid I'll fall down."

"You get used to it," Taylor said with a shrug. "Whyn't you start a fire and put some water on for coffee while I mix up the makings for some stick bread?"

"So it will be stick bread and jerky for lunch?" Hahn sighed. "Be still, my pounding heart."

"If you got something better in mind, I'm open to suggestion."

"In mind? Oh my, yes. A nice fillet of beef would be nice and a red wine sauce to go with it. New potatoes with parsley and butter. Fresh-picked lima beans. And an egg custard for dessert, I think. How would that be?"

Taylor smiled. "If you can cook it out here in the middle o' nowhere, I will damn sure eat it."

"Later perhaps. Right now I suppose we must settle for your stick bread and jerky."

"It has been said around many a campfire that I make the finest stick bread this side of San Francisco and never you mind that I'm the one that has said it. Now if you will excuse me . . ." He turned away and began unbuttoning his trousers.

* * *

"Y'know," Taylor mused as he dumped the last of the coffee into his cup, "I have t' give you credit for one thing." He stopped there and paid attention to the steaming coffee under his nose.

Unable to resist knowing what he was receiving credit for, Hahn rose to the bait. "What thing would that be, John?"

Taylor smiled. "You make the absolutely worst cup o' miserable damn coffee I ever drunk." Then he laughed. "But it's better than no coffee, ain't it?" He hesitated a moment and added, "I think."

"Bastard," Hahn said.

"Asshole," Taylor returned.

But neither of their voices held any venom.

Taylor yawned and stretched. "If we was up here for any normal reason I'd be wanting a little siesta about now."

"Siesta? What does that mean?"

"Rest. A little nap. Crawl onto that bed o' dry pine needles over there and stretch out for a while. But as it is . . ." He tossed the dregs of his coffee onto the coals of what had been their noonday fire, stretched again, and stood. "Time we bestir ourselves, Dick. We got serious stuff t' do and we've lost the better part of a day now thanks to that son of a bitch Ederle. Time we get back on the track of those kidnappers."

"I'll get the horses," Hahn offered.

* * *

Taylor reined wide around a sprawling fan of low-growing juniper. He had come to hate juniper. Damn things were just tall enough to hide a calf, or a cow if it was lying down, and they were a nuisance to get through. At the moment he was not thinking about how to chouse strays out of the brush, though. He was thinking about Jessica. And Loozy. And the happy life they once had.

Happy, anyway, for him. Jess must have been miserable and he had not seen it. Honestly had not. He wondered if she was happy with Dick Hahn.

He turned in his saddle and looked back at the dapper little man. It was not a question he could ask, of course. Certainly not of Hahn—who might well be as oblivious about that as John had been—and not of Jess either. But he wondered.

The truth was, he hoped she was happy. God, he loved her. Not as a possession but as a friend. And he missed her.

Missed Loozy too. Missed the sound of her incessant questions. Her childish laughter at the smallest of things. Her innocence. Loozy had seemed happy at home—his home; their real home—even if Jessica had not been.

He missed them both.

Hahn saw Taylor looking back at him and asked, "What is it, John?"

Taylor did not have time to answer. He felt a sudden burning on his side and a moment later heard the dull, echoing report of a rifle shot.

"Down," he shouted. "Get down. That bastard is shooting at us." He bailed out of his saddle, hit the ground hard, and bounced to his feet waving his arms to chase his horse and pack animal back up the canyon where they would be safe.

Hahn dismounted too and had the presence of mind to grab his shotgun before Taylor ran back and spooked those horses to chase after the ones Taylor had already sent running.

Both men dropped behind the spread of dark juniper as another rifle shot rang out.

Louise Taylor

Loozy sat on a boulder not far from the entrance to their . . . what was it called? Not a cave. She knew that. An . . . edit? No, adit. That was what the man said it was. They had been left in an adit with a few old burlap sacks for their bed and very little to eat. It was awful. But out here on the ledge with practically the whole world spread out below it was . . . beautiful. It really was.

Out here she could forget about everything except the beauty of these mountains and the immensity of the sky.

Loozy sat with her head tilted back and looked up at the bright blue and the few scudding white clouds like puffs of cotton sailing across the sky.

She saw an eagle soaring above the earth. Seeking prey, no doubt, but thrilling to watch, itself as beautiful as its surroundings. The eagle's wings rocked back and forth. Reacting to the wind? Possibly, she thought, feeling a light breeze against her cheek and the side of her neck. The eagle would be feeling those same breezes. She wondered if the great bird could appreciate the beauty of its surroundings.

Loozy sighed. Probably not, she conceded. Probably it felt only an impulse to hunt and to eat.

But was it possible that the eagle took joy in its ability to fly, to soar so far above the earth?

"Are you all right, baby?" She had not heard her mother come up beside her.

"Yes, Mama. I'm just . . . you know . . . sitting here."

"Come along now, please. We need to go down and collect some more wood. We've burned just about everything we brought up before."

"In a minute."

"No, ma'am, right now. I won't have you—"

"Mama."

"What is it now?"

"I wasn't saying no to you, Mama. It's that man. I see him, Mama. Down there." She pointed down the mountainside, past where they had gone to collect wood. "I see his horse. Look."

Jessica Taylor looked where Louise was pointing. She began to tremble. Loozy could see it and she could see the way her mama's breathing began to come hard. She slipped her hand into her mother's and squeezed, but the gesture did not seem to give comfort.

"It will be all right, Mama. It will be all right."

Jessica did not react to the words, but she did suddenly and quite fiercely hug Louise, then spin her around and propel her toward the opening to the old mine.

"Go inside, baby. Don't say anything or come out until I call you, you hear me? Not a word. Go now." She gave Loozy a little push to speed her on her way inside.

Loozy ran, frightened all over again now that the man was back.

Chapter 18

"Jesus God, John, you've been shot."

Taylor managed a grin. "I already knew that, Dick."

The two were lying underneath the spread of a low-growing juniper.

"You aren't bleeding much," Hahn said. He pushed Taylor's coat back and tugged his shirt out of his trousers, exposing a three-inch-long mark across his left side. "You haven't been, shot through, just sort of scraped."

"You say I'm not bleeding bad?" Taylor asked, unable or more likely unwilling to look for himself.

"It's seeping rather than running. Maybe it will help if I put something over it. To act as a bandage, you see." He let go of Taylor's shirt and allowed it to fall over the wound without regard to the bleeding.

"Do you have anything you could use for that?" It was one thing to get a little blood on his shirt. That happened frequently when he was working, especially when he was doing ranch work. But it was quite another to get blood on his coat. He did not like that.

"Not really. A kerchief, but I've blown my nose on it a couple of times." Hahn dug into his pocket and came out with a red and white paisley print square of cloth.

"Couple of times, hell. This thing has enough boogers on it to make a soup," Taylor said.

"You don't want it?"

"Hell, I guess it's better than nothing. Go ahead and use it."

Hahn held it up to the light and picked a few small, dark lumps off the cloth.

Taylor admired the cloth and chuckled, "Ah, at least my wound will be fashionably dressed."

Hahn pressed his handkerchief against the wound. "I don't have anything to bind it there."

"That's all right. I'll hold it in place. We won't be moving anywhere for a while."

"If you don't mind me asking," Hahn said, "what do we do now?"

"How the hell should I know? I've never been in any sort of gunfight before now."

"Me neither."

"I can tell you one thing," Taylor said. "The guy down there can't get to us without us hearing him come. We'll hear his footsteps on this gravel long before he reaches us. And you've got your shotgun for when he does. Which reminds me. Do you have any extra shells for that thing?"

"Lots of them—"

"Oh, good."

"—on my horse."

Taylor shrugged—and winced from the pain the gesture cost him—and said, "Okay, maybe not so good. But it is loaded, isn't it?"

"Yep. With buckshot."

"Then all we have to do is wait for him to come close and then you shoot him." He smiled. "Easy, eh?"

"Do you think it's that big fellow from back at Embry's store?" Hahn asked.

"Pretty much has to be," Taylor said. "He's the one sent us up here. He's the only person who knew where we'd be."

"He's already robbed us. What else does he want?" Hahn complained.

"The horses, I suppose. Those were stolen horses he sold to Embry. Phil as much as said so. I suppose he wants our horses and gear to sell next."

"The son of a bitch," Hahn growled.

"Quiet now. Quit your fidgeting," Taylor said. "If he hears us he'll know where we are."

"It isn't easy lying still on these old needles. They itch." As if to demonstrate the discomfort, Hahn reached underneath himself and scratched.

"Yeah but hold still anyway. He'll come after us. He has to if he wants our stuff." Taylor lay back and concentrated on holding the handkerchief against the scrape on his side. It was not a serious wound, but it hurt like a son of a bitch.

* * *

"Shh," Hahn whispered.

"I hear 'im," Taylor whispered back. "Hear that crackling sound? I think he's gotten himself into that mess of scrub oak down below us. Probably now he doesn't know how to get himself out without us hearing him."

"Well, let's hope he can't figure that one out," Hahn said with fervor.

"Shh."

"Sorry," Hahn said, this time again remembering to whisper.

* * *

Taylor rolled onto his right side. "You know what?" he whispered. "This rifle scrape doesn't hurt so bad now."

"Is it still bleeding?" Hahn asked.

"No. I don't think so." He peeled the bandana away

from the angry red blemish on his flesh and said, "I think it's all right now. Not all right, exactly, but it isn't seeping blood anymore. You want your handkerchief back?"

"You aren't even going to wash and iron it before you give it back?" Hahn was grinning when he posed the question.

* * *

"It will be dark soon," Hahn said. "Is that a good thing?"

"Not really." Taylor paused and considered the question. "I don't know."

"I wish I could stand up. I need to take a leak."

"Roll over on your side and let 'er rip. Just do it so it flows downhill."

"I might have thought of that on my own, but thank you for the suggestion."

"Always glad t' help."

"You're just lucky you aren't lying downhill from me."

Taylor chuckled and then became silent again.

* * *

"I hear him coming, John. Lord but I'm scared." It was dusk. In a matter of minutes would be dark.

"So am I, Dick."

"Do you think he's close enough? Should I shoot now?"

"Wait. Just wait a minute." Taylor came onto his hands and knees and began crawling through the juniper fans, shaking the dusty foliage and making more noise than was necessary.

"What are . . . oh, I see." Hahn pulled both hammers of his shotgun back into firing position, then reconsidered and let one down again so he had only one barrel cocked. That way he could not be frightened into firing both barrels at once and rendering them unarmed. He lifted himself onto one knee and winced as long-unused muscles rebelled.

Without warning, Taylor jumped upright, holding a rock in each hand. He threw one at the dimly seen figure about ten yards down toward the mouth of the fold in the mountainside; then he immediately dropped out of sight in the juniper bushes.

Their tormentor snapped a shot at the spot where Taylor had just been. By then Hahn had come up out of his crouch. He shouldered his scattergun as if he were wing-shooting pigeons and fired toward whoever was out there. The flame spewing from the muzzle of his shotgun lighted the brush for yards around, momentarily blinding Hahn. He immediately dropped back down into a crouch.

He heard thrashing below them, an animal—a human being, for instance—moving loudly and the crackling of brush.

Then there was silence.

He was still listening when the sun completely disappeared and the cloak of night spread over them.

Hahn wished Taylor had thought to come back close before it got dark. If Taylor was still alive, that is. The man with the rifle had fired at him. Taylor might be dead now for all Dick Hahn knew, and he did not dare call out and make a target of himself for the rifleman.

He huddled on the ground underneath the junipers, thoroughly miserable and feeling more alone than at any time in his life, clinging to the shotgun with its one remaining shell.

Ervin Ederle

Erv dropped a burlap sack of comestibles onto the floor and looked at what he had there. The woman and kid looked thoroughly miserable, unkempt, filthy, and bedraggled. He considered making them bathe—while he watched, of course, just to guard against any attempt to escape; that thought brought a grin to his face—but realized that might cause more problems than benefits.

For one thing, the air was chill at this elevation. Getting them wet could cause one of them to sicken and die, and he did not want that. Threats about one were his surest method of keeping the other in line.

The grown one, for instance. She did what he said, whatever he said, because he had convinced her that to do otherwise would cause him to transfer his attentions to the kid.

Later . . . he was still undecided about that. If the ransom was paid he just might let them go.

Or not.

It had rocked him down at Phil's store to discover that the banker was not the husband and father. That was the big cowboy. Erv had seen him around town, mostly in a saloon or talking with the loafers who hung around the mercantile. So the banker was a boyfriend. The sorry slut left her husband and was shacking up with the moneyman. She was even more of a snooty bitch than he thought. Now that he had thought about it, though, it really did not matter who she was screwing any more than it mattered who paid the ransom. Just so long as the ransom was paid. And it was enough to set him up in Mexico.

In his idle moments—and Erv had many idle moments, which was just the way he liked it—he was fond of speculating about how much ransom he could extract from the little banker. Fond too of thinking about what he would do with it. The tequila. The women. The easy life down South.

"There's some bacon in that poke," he announced to the females, who were cowering at the back of the dig. "Cook me up some of it. An' make me some 'pone with the cornmeal you'll find there. You do know how to make cornpone, don't you? Well, don't you?"

He waited until the woman nodded, then said, "I'm gonna bring up some more firewood. See that you have things ready by the time I get back."

Both the woman and the kid scurried after the burlap sack. They started pulling stuff out of it, including the mesquite smoked bacon that Erv doted on. That was his favorite, perhaps even better than elk liver.

He started down the hill to find dry wood.

Later . . . well, later he would send the kid back onto her bed while he took the woman around to the side of the ledge and had some fun with her. Now, that was something to look forward to.

Erv whistled a merry tune as he worked.

Chapter 19

"Jesus Christ, John, you scared the shit out of me." Hahn practically jumped out of his skin at Taylor's almost, but not quite, silent approach.

Taylor chuckled. "Why, Dick, I didn't know you knew words like that." The chuckle turned into a muffled laugh. "On the other hand, I damn sure do know that Jessie knows that one and a whole lot more."

"I wouldn't know about that," Hahn sniffed.

"You will." Taylor crawled beside Hahn and lay down.

"It will be daylight soon," Hahn said. "I can almost see my hands."

"The ones that're shaking?"

"Yeah, that would be them. Or, um, those. Whatever." Hahn paused, then asked, "Do you think he will be coming for us once it's light?"

"If I had to guess, yes, I'd think so. I know I would."

"He could just wait. Eventually we'll have to move. We'll have to go to water if nothing else."

"Or he will," Taylor suggested. "Listen for him. If you hear him moving, up and blast him."

"I'd rather he just go away."

"Maybe he will, Dick. Maybe he will."

"How is your wound this morning?" Hahn asked.

"It's dry now. Crusting over. I've had plenty worse than this. It will form a scab and a few weeks later be pretty much gone. A bullet might be scarier than a steer's horn, but they act about the same."

"Yes, but a bullet can kill you," Hahn said.

"So can a cow's horn."

Both men lay silent then on their bed of prickly juniper needles while the sun inched over the horizon and slid higher into the sky.

* * *

Taylor removed his hat and used the palm of his hand to wipe the sweat off his forehead. He whispered, "I wish I'd had forethought enough t' take this damn coat off before daybreak. Now I'm roasting."

"Before dawn it was too cold to take your coat off."

"I didn't say it was logical, but I am sayin' I got a right to complain."

"Why are we whispering?" Hahn asked. "He already knows we're here."

"Come to think of it, you're right," Taylor said in a normal speaking voice. He raised his voice into a shout and added, "Hey, you out there. You go to hell."

"Do you feel better now?"

Taylor grinned. "Yeah. I think I do. Try it."

"To hell with you, mister," Hahn shouted.

"And twice on Sunday," Taylor added just as loudly.

Hahn looked at him and raised his eyebrows. Taylor lifted his shoulders and held his palms upraised and empty.

"I got to take a leak again," Hahn moaned a little while later.

"Well, I know you don't got to go real bad this time because neither one of us has had a drop to drink in damn near forever."

"It feels bad."

"Then let me move outta the way. I don't want t' be downhill from the flood."

* * *

"Damn it, John, I can't stand much more of this. I just can't."

Taylor rolled onto his side and squinted up at the sun burning down on them, soaking them in sweat and aggravating their growing thirst. "I keep thinking of the water hanging on the sides of those horses up-canyon. I kinda wish one o' them would stray back down here, even if it meant the SOB down below shot it. Then I could crawl back to it and fetch us the water bag."

"With our luck," Hahn said, "the horse would drop with the water underneath it. Or you could get shot too."

"You're right. I should send you to retrieve the water."

* * *

Hahn rolled onto his side and looked up at the sun, which by now was at its zenith and would soon be starting down again. "John," he said, "you aren't as bad a man as I expected you would be. I'm sorry for all the things I've said about you."

"Hell, Dick, I bet they aren't a candle to what-all I've said about you."

"Yes, well, you have your reasons," Hahn conceded. He paused, then swallowed hard before he said, "Anyway, I just wanted you to know that. That I, um, misjudged you."

Hahn slapped Taylor on the shoulder, then stood, the shotgun cradled across his chest.

"Damn it, Dick, get down. Quick."

Hahn ignored him. He cocked the hammer over his last remaining shell and shouldered the gun; then with his eyes toward the place where they last saw the man who attacked them, the frail Hahn began walking slowly and deliberately down the canyon.

* * *

"John," Hahn called in a loud voice. "Come on down here. You should see this for yourself."

"It's safe?" Taylor asked before he rose from the junipers.

"Oh yeah, it's safe," Hahn returned.

Taylor scrambled out of the junipers and down the coarse rock and gravel bed of the narrow gulch where they had been trapped. "What is . . . oh." He stopped short, having to ask no more about what Dick Hahn had discovered.

The rider who called himself Randy Smith lay on his back, eyes and mouth wide open. His flesh had a waxy, yellowish cast to it. Beard stubble stood out in dark contrast to the pallor of his skin. A pool of congealed blood lay on the ground beneath him.

"It wasn't that big fella after all," Taylor said softly.

"No, it wasn't." Hahn sighed. "This fellow must have caught some pellets when I fired at him yesterday evening. I . . . feel rather strange about this. Knowing . . . you know. I shot a man. Actually shot someone."

"Jesus!" Taylor said. "You mean we been hiding out from a dead man all this time?"

"I suppose so. But we didn't know. It would have been foolish to take chances."

Taylor looked at him for a moment before saying, "Like

the chance you took when you came down here? You didn't know the son of a bitch was dead. It was a brave thing you done, coming after him like that."

Hahn shrugged. "He must have thought we had money on us. He wanted to rob us. Perhaps even kill us. I've never shot at a person before, but I'm not sorry about this. What are you doing, John?"

Taylor had dropped to kneel beside the dead man. "I'm checking his pockets and I'm taking his guns, that's what I'm doing. Do you want his rifle or the pistol? You take one; I'll keep the other." He thought about swapping his hat for Randy's. Randy's was newer and in better shape, but there was something about the idea of wearing the man's hat, with his sweat on the liner and the brim shaped to suit a dead man. That just did not sit well with him. He left the hat where it was. And he left the man's money in his pockets too. He would hate to have to think of himself as a thief. Taking the guns was only good sense, but taking money would feel like stealing.

"You can't . . . that is . . ." Hahn was clearly unhappy with the idea of taking anything at all.

"The son of a bitch is dead, Dick, and there's no law here to turn him over to. He for damned sure can't get any more use outta them guns and maybe we can. Now let me set them aside and we can drag him over to that cutbank yonder. We'll spill some dirt down on him an' let it go at that. Then if you don't mind you can hike up-canyon an' fetch our horses while I go look for his. We'll just add it to our string."

"Shouldn't we find someone to report this to?"

Taylor shook his head. "That's all the way down to town. It would take days, Dick. Maybe longer. Don't forget, every minute that goes by, Jessica and Loozy are in the hands of that gang o' kidnappers an' God knows what's happening to them. No, sir, we can't delay any longer'n we have to. Any reports that get done will have t' be after this is over an' we can go home. And if it comes to be that, we don't make it home again, well, then it won't matter anyhow."

"You're right, of course." Hahn hesitated, then went on, "I'll go find our horses and bring them down."

"I'll meet you . . . uh . . . not here. Not by all this blood. Down by that bend in the gulch. Now grab this fella's feet, will you? The quicker we get him covered up, the quicker we can get after them kidnappers again."

Jessica Taylor

Jessica wiped her nose on the hem of her dress. That would have been unthinkable just a few short days ago. Now it was . . . unimportant. As so very much was, it seemed. Loozy was important. Staying alive was important. When she thought about it, there was not very much more that was.

A bath. Now, that would be deeply, thoroughly, completely enjoyable. Would it be truly important? Probably not. But if they lived through this horrid experience, she intended to draw a bath and soak in it until she wrinkled up and looked like a prune.

Not that she expected ever to feel clean again. Not after that man, that awful man. He was crude and he hurt her and there was no water to spare for bathing. The water that came seeping out of the rock was icy cold and there was not enough of it to bathe in. The best she could do was to take a bit of cloth torn from her petticoat and sponge herself off. That was far from making her feel really clean. She wanted to take a scrub brush to all the places where he touched her.

Jessie began to cry again. She had thought her tears all used up. but it seemed that was something there was no end to.

Loozy came out of the cave—or whatever the miserable place was if it was not actually a cave—and said, "He says we should bring up some more wood and collect some water."

Jessica stood. She wiped her face with her palms and tried to dry her eyes. She made no attempt to hide the fact of her tears from Loozy. At this point those were far from being secret. Instead she sniffed and snuffled a little and managed a shaky smile for her daughter. "Look at the bright side. It gets us outside and away from him for a spell."

Loozy smiled. Too brightly perhaps, but then she was trying her best to put a good face on things also.

"Ready?"

The little girl nodded.

"Do you know that I love you?"

She nodded again.

"That's my girl. Now get the water bucket, please. We'll set it underneath that seep so it will be filling while we go down for the wood. And be careful on this ledge. It wouldn't do for either of us to fall." But it would be wonderful if the man took a tumble, Jess considered. Might it be possible to, well, to somehow arrange such a thing?

She startled herself with the thought and immediately rejected it.

But it kept coming back, circling at the fringes of her consciousness.

Then with despair another thought came to her. If they did somehow manage to rid themselves of the man, whatever would they do after that? They did not know where they were or how to find their way home from here. If something happened to the man, awful though he was, she and Loozy would be even worse off than they were now.

"Are you coming, Mama?" Loozy was standing at the top of the path giving her a questioning look.

Jessica returned a weak smile. "Right behind you, baby."

Chapter 20

"Anything?"

Taylor looked up at Dick Hahn, who was in the saddle while Taylor knelt beside an island of sandy dirt in an expanse of gravel. Taylor shook his head. "I'm afraid not."

"But I thought you said—"

"I said I saw something, damn it. I didn't say it was them. Hell, now that I look close I'm not even sure this was made by a horse. Could have been an elk. Could have been almost anything. It's only a scrape, not a print."

Hahn folded his hands over his saddle horn and leaned forward. His expression was pained and fearful. "What are we going to do? We have to find them, John. We just have to."

"I tell you true, Dick, I'm getting to the point of thinking we should go back down an' tell the sheriff. Maybe get a posse out after them."

"But the men who are watching to see if there is a posse," Hahn said. "What about them? The kidnappers said they would kill the girls if I tell anyone. It's bad enough that I told you. They would be sure to see if the sheriff swore in a posse."

Hahn straightened up and his eyes went wide. "Good Lord, man. One of the watchers could show up and ride with a posse and we would never know it. He could lead us all astray while his friends murder Jessica and Loozy."

"Aye, that's what worries me too, damn it."

"So what do we do now?"

"The only thing I can think of, Dick, is that you an' me go back to the last place we knew for sure we were onto their tracks. We'll start over from there."

"I don't even remember where that would be," Hahn groaned.

"Don't worry." John Taylor stood and gathered his reins before swinging up onto his horse's back. "I do."

* * *

Hahn nudged his horse up beside Taylor's. "Do you want to stop at the store?" he asked. He could see the roof about three-quarters of a mile ahead.

Taylor shook his head. "There's no need. We have all the food and things that we need. Besides, for all we know he might be the one who put that guy on our trail. I wouldn't trust Embry to have a second shot at us."

"Surely he wouldn't . . ."

"I didn't mean that t' be taken literally, Dick. I meant a second chance to set somebody after us. I don't think the fat man would have the nerve to do it himself, but we know he had dealings with that horse thief we met there. Fact is that I just wouldn't trust him."

"Yet you trusted that man at the . . . what did you call it? The hog ranch. You know. In that beautiful glen by the waterfall."

"Difference is that I know Nate. Know him well enough to have an idea how far we could trust him. Embry I don't know beans about an' what little I do know isn't very good what with him buying those stolen horses. If it's all the same to you, we'll ride on by Embry's store and head back up into the mountains."

"How far to where you lost their tracks?" Hahn asked.

"This afternoon. We'll get there this afternoon. It's going to be slow going after that, though."

"Why?"

"Because," Taylor said patiently, "that is where we lost the tracks. If they'd been easy to pick up from there, we wouldn't have lost them, would we?"

"Oh, I . . . see what you mean."

The packhorse Hahn was trailing swung its head aside and nipped one of the animals Taylor was leading. The two snorted and kicked and got the third led horse upset. Taylor spurred his horse ahead, dragging the led horses with him and putting a stop to the brawl before it became too serious. Hahn dropped back behind the animal they had claimed from the dead man and stayed there.

* * *

John Taylor stood in his stirrups and swiveled to look over his shoulder, right hand tight on the rein and left hand resting on his cantle. "Shit," he grumbled.

"Is there something wrong?" Hahn asked.

Taylor motioned him forward and said, "We got weather coming in, damn it."

"I brought a slicker. Surely you did too," Hahn said.

"It ain't the idea of getting wet that bothers me. I've rode in the wet pretty much all my life. What worries me is that if there's a hard rain it could cover over some of the tracks the kidnappers left."

Hahn's face drained of color. His whiskers, unshaven for several days now, stood out in hard contrast to the sun-reddened ruddiness of his skin. "Jessie," he whispered. "She could be lost to me."

"We could go back to town," Taylor said. "The note said

you had two weeks to put the ransom together. We could wait for the next note an' try to negotiate with them. See if they'd take what you got, what's yours to offer. I . . . I'd kick in whatever I could. It wouldn't be much. The rent money that I've saved up. That's about all I got. You could . . . I'd give it to you if it would do any good."

Hahn's eyes met Taylor's and held there for a moment; then he said, "I take that kindly, John. Very kindly indeed."

"Do you want to go back, then?"

"Now? No. Not yet anyway. We still have time. I say we should keep looking just as long as we can. We'll go back to Thom's Valley only if we absolutely must. If that's all right with you."

Taylor nodded and looked again at the sky where a line of low-hanging dark cloud was advancing. "Come along, then, Dick. Let's see can we find a place to hole up for tonight."

"Back at Embry's?"

"No," Taylor said with an emphatic shake of his head. "We aren't backtracking any more'n we have to. For now I got to think. Got to work out in my mind where these sons of bitches are going." His expression was grim. "An' how we can catch up to them before they hurt the girls."

"Whatever you think, John. I'm with you. I would feel comfortable negotiating with the gang, but out here . . . you've heard the expression 'babe in the woods'?" He grinned. "Well, out here it fits."

"Come on, then. Let's find a place to hole up before that storm gets here."

Ervin Ederle

Erv chewed the end of a twig until it was flat and used it to scrub his teeth. He had nearly all of his teeth left, a fact that he was proud of. When he was done cleaning his teeth, he tossed the twig into the fire burning just outside the mouth of the adit, rocked back on his heels, and sighed.

Tomorrow, he was thinking, tomorrow he might go down the mountain a little distance and see if he could find a deer or maybe an elk. Fresh liver would be a treat.

He stood, stepped out onto the ledge they were on, and unbuttoned his trousers. While he urinated over the edge, he stared down at the tops of some black cloud that had swirled in. Likely it was raining down there. Up on the ledge it had gotten colder thanks to the moisture in the air that made the rock walls clammy. If the rain crawled up this high, it would turn to snow and make the footing treacherous.

Erv finished his business, tucked himself in, and buttoned his fly. He would be wanting the woman again later, but it was too cold to do anything with her outside. Better to send the kid out instead. Or let the kid watch; he didn't care.

He pulled his calendar stick out of his pocket and counted off the days since he had taken his hostages. He had time before he started down to get his ransom. If nothing else he needed to make sure the husband and the whatever the hell the little one was had plenty of time to quit screwing around looking for him and get back to town. He wanted to make sure they had the ransom money ready and waiting for him.

Lordy, how much would it be? Several thousand. Surely there would be that much. Five thousand? Ten? He was eager to find out. But not foolhardy. Not Ervin Ederle. Never foolhardy.

He pondered again on what he should do with the woman and the kid when he went down to get the ransom.

It would be good to be able to display them alive and well as an inducement for the two pilgrims to turn over the money.

But it would not be necessary. He was fairly sure about that. He could just collect first and promise them delivery afterward.

And of course once he rode away from Thom's Valley with all that cash in his saddle pockets, he would have no use for the woman and the kid one way or the other.

He was not going to take them with him to Mexico. He had decided that firm as firm could be. The woman was too prissy and she was sure to be teaching the kid to be the same way. So no, that was definitely out.

The question now was whether he should take them with him when he went down to the town. On the one hand, it would push things in his favor if he could show them before he collected his money. On the other, it would be a risk. They might be seen. Might somehow get away from him down there where they would know where they were and know they could find their way home on their own.

No, he decided now, they would have to remain up here when he left. He chuckled. He pretty much had to leave them here. After all, he had already sold their horses.

He pondered a little longer, then grunted. Dead, he thought. It would be better to leave them dead. If he tied them up they would just lie there and slowly starve to death, as he damned sure was not going to come all the way back up here once he got the banker's money.

Erv did not want to do that. It would be cruel to let them starve, and he did not like to think of himself as a cruel man. It would be much better—much kinder to them and safer for himself—to put them out of their misery before he left.

He nodded and gave a soft but emphatic grunt. He would do them the kindness of shooting them before he went down to get the money.

His expression spread into a grin.

He would shoot them then. But in the meantime . . .

He turned and walked back into the adit. The two were lying tight together, twined like two strands of a flat braid. They were not sleeping, though. He was sure of that.

He reached out a boot toe and poked the kid in the ribs. She sat up. "Yes, sir?"

"I want you t' go outside. Just hang around out there 'til I call you back in. You understand me?"

"Yes, sir, I think so."

"Go on now. I'll call you when I want you."

The kid trotted obediently outside. The woman looked up at him with a look of raw disgust. Not that he gave a damn.

Erv began unbuttoning his fly.

Chapter 21

"Hurry up, Dick. Build us a fire underneath the overhang of them tree branches and drag in some extra wood. I think we're gonna need it," Taylor said, digging into the pack on the horse he had been leading.

Taylor strung a rope between two stout saplings, pulling it as tight as he could, and tied all five horses to it facing with their butts to the rising wind. He unsaddled his own horse, Hahn's and the spare that had belonged to Randy whatever-his-name-was, then pulled the packs on the other two. He stuffed the saddles and filled packs under the trees where Hahn was still fussily trying to get a fire started.

"I wish we had a tarpaulin with us," Taylor said, looking up into the heavily needled branches that provided a shelter of sorts. "That'd shed water a whole helluva lot better than these branches will." He knelt to give Hahn a hand with the fire, then sat back onto his haunches as the first flames began to rise in response to the smaller man's efforts.

"Y'know, Dick, I think you're beginning to get the hang of this outdoor livin'," he said with a grin.

"I shall take that as a compliment, John."

"Good. That's how I meant it." He inched closer to the fire and spread his hands to warm them.

The first wind-driven raindrops began to fall.

* * *

"Lord, I hope Jessie and Louise are indoors somewhere and not out in this miserable weather," Hahn said.

John Taylor poured a cup of steaming coffee for himself and offered a refill to Hahn, who shook his head no. Taylor lifted the cup beneath his nose and inhaled deeply, then said, "You really do care for them, don't you?"

"Of course I do."

"Jessica is an awful good-looking woman, and . . . forgive me for sayin' this . . . I always thought you just wanted to bed my wife. I didn't think you really cared for her. Didn't think you cared anything at all for Loozy. I was wrong."

"Thank you for saying that, John. And thank you all the more for seeing it. I . . . this situation must be hard on you. Mind if I change my mind about that coffee?" He held his cup out and Taylor poured it full. "To tell you the truth, I hadn't given thought to how Jess moving in with me would affect you."

"I still love her, Dick."

Hahn sighed. "So do I, John. God help us, so do I."

* * *

"I guess this just about ruins our chances of tracking them any farther," Hahn said as he pulled his cinch snug around the belly of the paint horse. He dropped the stirrup, checked on the lead rope on the packhorse, and swung onto the saddle, the movement sure and easy now unlike the awkward climb he had made just a few days earlier.

"What? The rain?" Taylor was already mounted and waiting. "Not as much as you might think. Lower down, like in the valley where they moved through grass, that rain would've hurt us bad. It would've pounded the grass flat or caused it to spring back. Same thing on soft ground. The rain would've washed out any marks they left. But up here it might be different."

Taylor reached forward and smoothed the mane of the brown. "Up here the ground is mostly gravel and hard clay. Or solid rock. On the clay the rain might actually fill in any places where a hoof has pressed into the soil. That actually makes a mark easier to see. An' on stone, the rain won't have wiped out any serious scrapes. We'll still be able to see them."

Taylor took up his reins and nudged the brown in the ribs. "We ain't done yet," he called over his shoulder. "I still figure to find them sons of bitches."

Jessica Taylor

Jessica eased around the puddle of rainwater that had accumulated near the mouth of the adit. The wind-driven mountain rain had been exhilarating. Wild and exciting. Now in the dawn the air smelled clean and fresh and new.

Behind her at the back of the adit, dear Loozy slept, the man snoring vigorously at her side. Jess felt alone now but not at all lonely. If it were not for the man, she would like it up here, like it very much. She was beginning to understand the pleasure John had always taken in the untamed country that surrounded the town. He spoke of it often, but she had never really understood it until now.

Jess walked out onto the ledge and peered down at the mountainside below, the naked rock above timberline, and the dark green of the wooded slopes below that demarcation. It was beautiful in these mountains. Beautiful in a way she had never experienced before now. If it were not for that awful man, she could be happy up here.

That fact startled her. Jessica always thought of herself as a cut above the common folk down in Thom's Valley.

Well, there was nothing to say she could not enjoy the beauty of nature and still be . . . special.

She knew she was pretty. Perhaps even beautiful.

But not here.

God, she had not bathed or even properly washed her face in days. Did not have so much as a comb or brush to take the knots out of her hair. It was a very good thing she did not have a mirror. Looking at Loozy, though, was enough to give her an idea of how tangled and unkempt she must be.

She would welcome that—would deliberately slap mud on herself and frizz her hair into a Medusa-like mess—if she thought for an instant that a terrible appearance would keep that vile man away from her.

She shuddered, hoping against hope that she did not become pregnant now. Loozy was proof enough that she was capable of bearing a child. Or had been. She and Dick had had no luck in that regard. Now . . . the thought was almost too much to bear.

Deliberately she pushed that unhappy thought away and stood straight and tall, her shoulders back. She drew the brisk dawn air into her lungs and tasted the cool freshness of it.

But her thoughts kept straying. Back to Loozy. Back to the fact that she would do whatever she had to, endure any pain, accept any humiliation, if only it would protect Louise.

Without warning, Jessica began to cry, her tears falling slow and soft and making pale tracks on her cheeks.

Where were they? Where were Dick and John and the posse of searchers who were sure to be down there somewhere? Why had they not come to find them?

Her tears came harder and her shoulders began to shake with her sobbing.

Where?

Chapter 22

Taylor stepped down from the saddle and stretched, trying to loosen his back. Dick Hahn got down and joined him. The two stood staring at the mountains that surrounded them, rugged slopes rising toward even more rugged peaks so high they were bare of vegetation, one after another like whitecapped waves on a choppy ocean.

"What do you think, John?"

Taylor did not speak immediately. He weighed his words carefully. And his thoughts with even greater care. "They're out there somewhere, Dick. Maybe being treated bad. They're . . . you know how vulnerable a woman is. Especially with men like those kidnappers must be. They know they're risking their lives for this. Any decent man who gets hold of them will hang the bastards as quick as he'd swat a horsefly. The kidnappers already have nothing to lose by . . . you know." Taylor's voice broke as he thought about what Jessica . . . and Loozy too for all he knew . . . might be going through.

"I've thought about that," Hahn admitted. "A lot."

Taylor gave him a searching look. "And . . . ?"

Hahn's chin rose and he pulled his shoulders back. "I don't care. I love her. Both of them. Whatever is happening now is not their fault. Whatever they have to do in order to survive, I'll not hold it against them. Anything!"

Taylor nodded. "Yeah. Kind of like I still love the both o' them after Jess went with you."

"You could say that, so yes, very much like your feelings have been." Hahn paused. He turned his head away and added, "I'm sorry, John. Sorry to have caused you that pain. I was thinking about Jess. I never gave thought to what you were going through. Now . . ." He shrugged.

Taylor cleared his throat and dropped some spittle between the toes of his boots. "Now we both want t' get them back. That's all that really matters right now."

"We can agree on that, John. Absolutely. Anything else that might be between us, well, Jessica and Loozy come first. Then we can think about those other things."

* * *

"I think I recognize where we are."

"Where we are, Dick, is the last place that I'm for sure we were on the kidnappers' track." He pointed to a slope where a faint wildlife trail wound its way up an expanse of gravel and red clay. "They must've gone up there. I didn't see sign. That's why I took us off that way," he said, pointing. "I was wrong."

"Now what do you think?"

"I think they did go up there. I just missed seeing it. I mean . . . we been down that way. We didn't get so much as a sniff of them. So from this point . . . if they went over that way, they would've been past Nate's place and he's sure to've seen them. So okay, they didn't go that way."

Taylor pointed farther to the north and said, "There's a pass over there. Not too hard a one. I helped Wynn Greaves bring some cows across it a couple years ago. That's why I looked so hard t' see could I find any trace of them over there."

"We were over that way?"

Taylor chuckled. "You don't know?"

"John, I've been lost pretty much all the time since we left the valley. I have no idea where we've been."

"Well, trust me. We've looked over there and there wasn't no sign of them." He turned and pointed toward the southwest. "If they'd went that way, they would've passed Embry's place. Apparently they didn't do that." He faced west. "Which leaves us looking up there."

"You sound unhappy about that," Hahn said.

"That's 'cause I for damn sure am. That's poor country up there. All the way up above timberline and no pass through to the other side."

"You've been up there?"

Taylor shook his head. "No, but I've spoke with some boys who tried to find a way across. They said they couldn't get through. It's too far from town for anybody t' be running cattle up there. Too steep in parts too. A fella might use it for summer graze if he was herding goats or something, but no cowman is interested."

"But the kidnappers could be up there?"

He nodded. "It's just possible."

"So we will look for them there?"

"That we will, Dick." Taylor gathered his reins and swung into the saddle. Hahn mounted as well.

"Lead the way, John."

Taylor nudged his brown into motion, the led horses following, and Hahn fell in behind.

* * *

"Damn it to hell," Hahn grumbled as they drew rein at a dead end. For more than two hours they had been following a game trail, but now that petered out at an expanse of loose scree where a rock slide had taken place sometime in the past. "Could we get down and rest a little while, John? My thighs are hurting." He managed a weak smile. "I don't know how you do it, staying in the saddle for days on end."

"You think I don't get sore too? Course I do, though maybe not so bad as you. I just don't bitch about it." Taylor grinned. "Not out loud anyhow. But sure. Git down. No point not to." He led by example, dismounting on the uphill side of the brown instead of the supposedly correct left-hand side of the horse.

"There's some small brush up the hill there, Dick. Whyn't you gather a little of it so's we can brew some coffee? I don't know 'bout you but I could surely use a cup. It's colder'n hell up this high. Makes me wish I had brought me a bearskin coat, but I sure never thought to." He began digging into the pack carried by the horse Dick Hahn was leading, looking for their pot and cups and into his own packs for their water bag. Half an hour later they had a small fire blazing and a pot of water over it heating to make the coffee.

"That will take a few minutes," Taylor said. "I dunno why but up this high it seems a boil isn't as hot as 'tis down lower. Takes for-damn-ever to make coffee up here."

Hahn nodded and wandered off to take a leak. He was examining the rock slide when his eyes went wide and he yelped, "John. Come quick!"

Taylor leaped to his feet and ran to Hahn's side. Hahn merely pointed to the rocky mountainside at their feet.

"Well, I'll be damned," Taylor mumbled. "Good going, Dick. Mighty good."

There on the stone was a pale scrape, a mark that could not have been made by the soft hoofs of the mountain sheep and wild goats that foraged at this elevation. It was a mark made by an iron shoe. Horses had passed this way and there was the proof.

"Dick, you've found them. Damned if you didn't."

Louise Taylor

Loozy held a tin cup under the slow trickle of snowmelt that came from the mountainside above them. The packed snow was crusted over with so much ice that even the rain did not wash it away, but there was seepage from underneath as the above-freezing air temperatures eroded the accumulation.

The cup gradually filled and she took a drink, the water so cold it took her breath away and made her teeth hurt. She drank again, then held the cup against the rock once more to refill it. When the cup was full she carried it back to the adit.

"Here, Mama." She handed the cup to her mother, then dropped to a seat on the cold stone floor.

"Thank you, baby." Her mother set the metal cup over a tiny fire to heat.

"Are you making coffee? Can I have some?"

"I'm not making coffee and you are much too young anyway."

"Mama!"

"I mean it. No coffee for you, young lady. Not until you are eighteen years old."

"That isn't fair."

"Possibly sixteen. We'll talk about that when the time comes. Which is not now." She moved the cup aside, added a little dry wood, and put the cup back in place.

"Do you think the man will . . . you know."

"Kill us? No, sweetie. Your daddy Dick will come pay

the ransom the man wants and he will let us go." She smiled. "You'll see. We will be fine."

"Promise?"

"Yes, baby. I promise."

Loozy suspected her mother was just trying to comfort her. But that was all right. It was good to be comforted. "I wonder if Daddy knows," she said. "I bet he's looking for us if he does know."

"You mean Daddy John? Yes, I'm sure he would be looking for us if he knows."

"If you aren't making coffee, what do you want with that water?"

Jessica stuck a finger into the cup to check the temperature, then said, "I need to wash myself. Be a good girl now if you please. Go outside and watch the path. If you see the man coming back, run and let me know. Will you do that for me, please?" Jessica picked up the cup of now warm water, turned her back, and lifted the hem of her dress.

Loozy went out onto the ledge and watched the trail below, shivering as a rising breeze sent the cold biting deep into her very bones.

For no reason she could think of she began to cry.

Chapter 23

"That is one helluva lousy footpath," Taylor said, eyeing the rock spill that had come down from higher up on the mountainside. "One false step an' you could go down. Be crushed by the rocks that'd come down with you." He turned to Dick Hahn and grinned. "But if those sons of bitches could make it, then so can we."

Hahn nervously looked ahead along the track they intended to take. "Right," he said uncertainly, as if to reassure himself more than to agree with Taylor. "Right. If they can, we can. And if the girls are over there, well, that's where we want to go."

Taylor hunkered down with his elbows on his knees and stared out across the expanse of loose scree, his brow knitted in thought. Finally he stood. "All right, Dick, here's what I think we need to do. I'll go over first an' show you how it's done.

"I think it's best to turn the horses loose an' let them pick their own way. I'll take the lead ropes off the packhorse and Randy Smith's horse so if one of them falls it won't take the others with it. And I'll get behind them until we're across. That way if one o' them spooks, it won't be runnin' into me and taking me down with it. You understand?"

Hahn nodded. "That makes sense."

"You wait here until we're across onto solid ground again; then you start your animals over. Mind you untie the lead rope on your packhorse. Don't worry about trying to lead them. They'll naturally want to come over to where the other horses are. Will be by then, that is. They'll want to join up with the others. All you got to do, Dick, is get them started on the path; then you hang back and follow along. Be careful about that, though. You could slip on those loose rocks an' fall just as easy as a horse could."

"Right."

"You want a swallow o' that coffee before we try this?"

"Yes, I . . . I think that would be a good idea."

Taylor smiled and clasped Hahn's shoulder. "Don't be worrying about it. Careful does it, but if those kidnappers could take God knows how many horses across there, then so can we."

"You don't mind if I pray a little about that, do you?" Hahn said, feigning lightness but meaning every word of it.

"Hell, Dick, I think that'd be a good idea. Now let's have us a bit o' coffee and put everything back in the packs. Oh, and something else I just now thought. You and me probably oughta carry our guns with us so if a saddle horse does go down we won't be out here naked. We might have a hard time of it trying to take down a kidnap gang and us with nothing to shoot."

* * *

Exhibiting more confidence than he really felt, Taylor led the brown over to the start of the treacherous path. He pulled Hahn's shotgun from the pouch that hung from his saddle, then unfastened the lead rope from his saddle horn. He gave the brown a swat on the rump to get it moving.

He untied the reins of the spare animal from the pack frame and let first one and then the other of those horses follow along behind the brown as they were by now well accustomed to doing. Neither horse hesitated.

"See, Dick? Dead easy."

"If it's all the same with you, I'd just as soon you didn't use that word right now."

"And, uh, which word would that be?"

Hahn smiled. "Dead."

That got a laugh out of Taylor, who started off behind the horse that had belonged to the would-be robber.

Dick Hahn led his paint forward. He stood indecisively for a moment, worrying over whether he should carry the rifle or his own fine shotgun. The shotgun, he concluded. It was worth more than a hundred fifty dollars while the common-as-grass rifle could be had for a pittance, so he left the rifle on his saddle and pulled the engraved and inlaid shotgun from its scabbard.

The paint was indeed eager to follow the others. All he had to do to get it moving was turn it loose.

The packhorse brushed past him and was out onto the spill of loose rock before he had time to unfasten it from the paint. If one of them fell, they both would go down.

Silently grumbling about forgetting that instruction, Dick Hahn followed close behind the butt of the packhorse.

Too close, as it turned out.

Once they were well out onto the talus, the pack animal became annoyed. It lashed out with both hind legs.

Hahn quickly ducked away. And lost his footing.

He fell, sliding down the mountainside and bringing tons of rock down with him. "Help! Help me, John."

Ervin Ederle

Ederle leaned back against the wall, unmindful of the cold that seeped from the stone directly into his bones. He was thinking of warmth. The warmth of yellow sun and brown women.

He would get at least two of them, he decided now, looking at the fancy bitch and her whelp. Two little Mexican girls to keep him comfortable. Two at all times. And if he got tired of one or they started giving him any lip, why, he could replace them just as easy as—he glanced around him and smiled—easy as falling off a mountain.

That life would happen just as soon as he collected his ransom.

And that would happen in just a few more days.

It would soon be time to head back down to Thom's Valley and slip another note to the banker fellow. Time for him to pay up. For nothing, of course, but he would not know that until it was too late.

By now the little bastard and his friend—who the devil would have thought that the woman was married to somebody else?—should be back down there getting the ransom money together.

Those two were motivated. Yes, sir, they damn sure were. They wanted the woman and girl back. They didn't know that was not going to happen.

Erv chuckled a little at that thought. He touched the gutta-percha grips of his revolver. He would be kind, he thought. He would shoot them while they slept. The woman first, then the kid. But not yet. He still had uses for the woman, and having the kid gave him control over the woman. It all worked out quite nicely.

Erv yawned and let the woman and her kid slide out of mind. He thought instead about what he would do with all that money, beyond the Mex women and the beer, that is. He might travel a little. See the ocean, even.

He had never seen the ocean and supposed it was like Lake Tahoe, which was the biggest lake he ever saw, except even bigger. He imagined it rimmed with high rock walls, blue and cold and sparkling where the sun struck it. He could sit up on one of those big old rocks and have his Mex girls fetch bottles of cerveza all day and half the night. Every day and every night. Now, wasn't that something to think about!

Erv smiled and scratched himself, not at all caring if the woman or the kid saw where he was scratching. They really did not matter. Both of them would be dead in just a few more days.

Chapter 24

"Help! Help me, John."

Taylor turned and watched with horror as Dick Hahn slid down on a cascade of rock and billowing dust, finally coming to a precarious halt well down the mountainside.

"Hang on, Dick. Don't move. Whatever you do, don't move no more."

He needed . . . damn, he needed rope. Lots of rope. All he had was an old maguey lariat that he used as a picket rope for the horses. That and . . . what? Damn it!

"Hang on."

"I am not going anywhere," Hahn shouted back.

"Can you . . . is there solid purchase where you stopped?"

"I'm afraid to move enough to find out."

"Did you bust anything?"

He could see Hahn shake his head. "I don't think so."

"Don't move now, Dick. We'll get you up."

Somehow, Taylor thought to himself.

But he had no idea how that would be.

* * *

Hahn looked like he was a long way down there, certainly too far down for the picket rope to reach him. Taylor gathered up Hahn's horses and tied them close to his own, then began looking for a way to extend the reach of that old lariat.

The packs. Of course. The lashings that held the packs in place. Those would help. And the dead man's saddle had a picket rope and an iron picket pin hanging off the pommel. That would do. He would put that so the metal pin was at the tip end of whatever he put together. That would give it weight to get it down to Hahn and be something Dick could grab on to once it got there.

Sure. They could do it. He began stripping the packs and tying everything together.

* * *

"Can you reach it?" It had taken three tries, but now he had pretty much gotten the hang of getting the makeshift line all the way down to Hahn. This time the line had fallen only a few feet to the left of the little man.

"Yeah." He reached. Stretched. Then he smiled. "Yeah, I've got it."

"Hold on to the picket pin, Dick. It should take your weight."

"Should? Did you say it should hold me?" His voice sounded like it came from far away.

"If I'm wrong about that, you're welcome to sock me one," Taylor shouted back.

"Thank you ever so much."

"Any time. D'you have hold of the picket pin now?"

"Yes, I do."

"All right, then. I'm not sure how far I trust this assortment of ropes and cords and such, so you climb as best you can while I pull from up here. Give me a second, though. I need to get myself braced so's I don't slide down there next to you."

Taylor set his feet and leaned back so he was more

lying against the slope of the mountain than he was standing upright. He took a firm hold on the rope and a deep breath to go with it, then started pulling. "Now, Dick. Now."

Jessica Taylor

A pang of sudden fear . . . no, more like terror . . . clutched at Jessica's throat and tightened like iron bands around her heart. The way the man was looking at her was one thing, but the way he glowered at Loozy was worse.

Anything he did to her, well, she was a grown-up. She could accept it. But Loozy . . . Jessica would spend her last drop of blood to save her daughter. The terrible thing was that she was beginning to believe she would have to do exactly that. And that she might fail even so.

She knew something was going on with the man, the ugly, disgusting, evil man. He was even rougher than before. He treated her now like something to be used and then discarded.

How many times had she seen a man smile with pleasure as he shoved a plug of fresh tobacco into his jaw only to spit it out once the juices were gone? Now Jess knew what it felt like to be that soggy lump. Or so she told herself.

This man did not even admit to any pleasure when he chose to exercise his control over his captive. He just did as he wished and then turned away without so much as a softening of his facial expressions.

And this was the man who held Loozy's well-being in his hands.

She felt something warm press against her side. She looked down to see Loozy's sweet curls. Jess extended her arm over Loozy's shoulders and pulled the child close.

"Why are you crying, Mama?"

"Am I? I didn't realize." She forced a smile. "There. Is that better?"

Louise buried her face against her mother's breast and she too began to weep.

Chapter 25

Dick Hahn's legs were trembling so bad he had to sit down. But not until he reached safe, solid ground. "That was . . . unpleasant."

"Yeah, you looked kinda uncomfortable down there."

"I was. Thank you for saving my life."

"It wasn't that big a deal."

"Oh yes, it was."

Taylor shrugged and said, "You lost your fancy shotgun."

Hahn blinked. "I suppose I did, didn't I? Funny. Until you mentioned it I didn't even notice." He stood, walked very carefully over to the edge of the rocky avalanche chute, and peered down the mountainside. "I don't see it, do you?"

"No, an' if I did it wouldn't make no difference. Dunno about you but I wouldn't go down there after it if the damn thing was made of solid gold." He grinned. "'Cept in that case I might come back with some serious hoists and stuff."

Hahn shivered. "It isn't worth a man's life, I can tell you that. Not yours, nor mine, either one."

"Looka here now, it's near on to dark. Whyn't we find us a good place to lay out our blankets? I'll start a fire and get us some coffee brewing. You set there and get your legs back under you. We'll go to looking again in the morning." Taylor's grin flashed again. "In the meantime, hand me that picket rope. If you're done using it, that is."

Hahn looked startled. He dropped his gaze to his hands, which continued to clutch at the iron picket pin from Randy's saddle. "I didn't realize . . . Here." He thrust the pin out toward Taylor and stared blankly into the darkening sky.

* * *

Dick Hahn squeezed his eyes tight shut and slowly shook his head back and forth. "I'm frightened, John. What if we don't find them? What am I to do? I can't pay all that ransom. I can't destroy an entire town. But what if the kidnappers won't accept my savings and go on their way?"

"If you're going to speculate, Dick, try to think about what if we find out where the kidnappers are holding them. Think about what if we get them safely back." He smiled and reached out to touch Hahn's shoulder, gently rocking him back and forth. "Hell, man, then I can go back to hating your rotten guts. We'd be just like nothing happened."

Hahn opened his eyes and looked at him. "I wouldn't blame you if you did, John. You really love them. I understand that now that they have been taken from me too."

"Yeah, Dick. An' I accept that you really love the both o' them too."

"You already know that I'm sorry about all of this. Hurting you, I mean. But . . . there are some things that fact does not change. I won't willingly send them back to you."

"No, I reckon you wouldn't. No more'n I'd send them to you."

Hahn gave him a small, sad smile. "Hell of a mess, isn't it?"

"Yeah. Yeah, damn it, it is."

"Pour me a little more of that coffee, would you?"

* * *

Taylor grunted as he stood. "Too much coffee," he said. "Now I gotta take a piss. An' I just went a few minutes ago."

"Then move along, big man. I don't want you to splash any of it on me."

"There was a time . . ."

Hahn laughed. "Yes, I know. You would have loved a chance to do exactly that."

"No more, though, Dick. Not no more." Taylor stepped well away from the fire, stood with his legs wide, and opened his fly. He started urinating and idly lifted his eyes toward the dark bulk of the mountain looming above them.

"Jesus!" he yelped.

Hahn leaped to his feet. "What? What is it?"

"I found them, Dick. I think I've found them."

"Wha—"

"Up there," Taylor said, pointing and practically aquiver with excitement. "See there?"

"I see a bright star," Hahn said.

"No, damn it, you don't. That dark patch is mountain, not cloud, and the bright speck is the reflection off a fire, not a star. I'd swear to it. That has to be them, Dick. That has to be where the kidnappers are holed up with Jess and Loozy."

"Oh my gosh. We . . . get your saddle, John, we'll—"

"No, we won't," Taylor interrupted. "We know where to go, more or less, but not until daybreak. You damn near died today falling down that rock slide. Don't take a second shot at it by trying to run up there in the dark."

"You're right. I know you're right. But . . . don't expect me to get any sleep tonight."

"Me too, damn it. Me too."

* * *

Taylor rolled over onto an elbow. He began chuckling.

"What the devil are you laughing about, John?" Hahn asked, his head under his blankets to keep the night chill off.

"It just now occurred t' me, Dick, that I think this is the day I'm s'posed to be in court answering that summons you sent."

"Oh, good Lord." Hahn sat up, his blanket falling away. "I completely forgot about that."

"So had I 'til just now. I suppose I'm in contempt now."

"I . . . I . . . I'm sorry, John. I'll straighten it out when we get back down."

"If you feel like it," Taylor said. He lay back down. "Go on now, Dick. Try and get some sleep. You might need it tomorrow."

"Good night, John. Again."

Ervin Ederle

Erv sat up and shook his head back and forth to clear the sleep from his brain. The woman and the kid were still sleeping, never mind that it was cold in the back of the adit. The fire had gone out and there was no more wood or dung to build it up again. He would have to send the two females down the mountain to collect some more dry blowdown or some old horse apples.

No, he thought with a chuckle, he would send just the kid down to collect the makings for a fire. The woman could stay up here and give him a little morning loving.

He stood and stretched, then walked out to the edge of the ledge. He spat over the side, unbuttoned his fly, and took a leak, then stood for a moment looking at an eagle that was soaring overhead.

Soaring free. That was how he would feel once he had that ransom money in hand and could head for Mexico. Free for life. And a mighty good life it would be too. Beer and women and the world at his feet. He smiled, thinking about it, thinking about all he could look forward to.

Maybe today he should head back down there to demand the ransom money from the little banker fellow. Why wait? Unless the little bastard was still wandering around looking for his woman . . . no, that big man's woman but in the little one's bed, and wasn't that something? . . . down at Phil's place where he had no business being.

It would serve them right, both of them, when they

found out they paid all that money for nothing because by then the woman and the girl would be dead.

Erv knew that was something he would have to do. For his own safety he had to shoot them. If he did not and they identified him . . . if someone came after him, whether with the law or just with a gun . . . no, for his own safety and his own peace of mind, they had to go.

But the truth was that it was something he did not look forward to. He had never killed a woman before, much less a little girl. That was serious. Just about as serious as it could get.

Now that he was close to the time of having to do it, he was getting a little nervous about it.

But, damn it, it had to be done. Had to.

He almost wished he still had his gang so he could order someone else to do the actual shooting. It would almost be worth splitting the ransom so he could give that order and not have to pull the trigger himself.

Erv sighed. A man does what he has to do and that is all there is to it. He does what he must.

The eagle had gone out of sight, around to the other side of the mountain. Erv walked back inside the open mouth of the adit. He was cold and they needed something to start a fire with. It was time to wake the woman and the kid.

Chapter 26

"How much farther?" Hahn stopped, leaned over, and rested his hands on his knees. He sucked at the thin air as if he could not get enough of it. "I'm . . . I'm light-headed. Almost dizzy," he puffed.

"It's the elevation," Taylor told him. "They say you get used to it if you stay up this high long enough. Personally I wouldn't know. An' don't want to stay here long enough to find out."

"They have to be close now, don't they?" He straightened up and wiped his nose with the back of his hand.

Taylor looked up the slope and said, "We're just about to the tree line. I figure that fire last night must've been above that, otherwise the light would've been blocked by the trees. And there aren't too many trees higher than where we are now."

Taylor was staring up toward the mountaintop. He brought his attention back down when Hahn said, "John."

"Mmm?"

"Over there, John. I see something. I don't think it's another elk."

Taylor rose in his stirrups and shaded his eyes against the glare of the still rising sun. "Hot damn!"

"What is it? Is it an elk?"

"That's a horse, Dick." His expression darkened and he added, "It's only one horse. Where are all the others?"

"They might have gone down to town to deliver another note," Hahn suggested.

"So why would they leave just one horse up here? And why wouldn't we have passed them on our way up?"

"Just one of them stayed behind to watch over Jessie and Louise? I mean, it's just a guess but . . ." He shrugged his shoulders.

Taylor scratched his face. The accumulation of beard there was itching. "That would be a break for us if it's true." He stopped climbing and reined across the slope toward the brown horse cropping grass in a copse of fir trees. "Damn," he said.

"What's wrong?" Hahn asked.

"That horse. I've seen it before."

"That one?"

"That's right. It belongs to that big fella . . . I don't remember his name . . . the one we saw down at Embry's place."

"Ederle," Hahn said. "His name is Ederle. Erv, I think." His lips pulled into a thin line and he said, "He's the bastard who stole my money. I'd bet on that." He grunted. "I'm not likely to forget that man." Hahn turned his head and spat. "Bastard!"

"He's also the one who claimed he saw six men and two women riding southwest, but there was no kind of trail left by any such a crowd, not that I could see. I'm thinking that he lied about that and took your purse. Bastard was having fun with us."

"But the girls," Hahn said. "Where are the girls?"

"If he's left his horse down here . . . and we saw fire up above timberline . . . they can't be far, Dick. I think we should ought to picket our animals an' walk up from here."

Hahn went back to the side of the paint horse and pulled the rifle from his saddle scabbard.

* * *

"I don't see anything," Dick Hahn said. They were standing on a faint trail that led beneath a long, narrow ledge. A trickle of snowmelt darkened the rock at one end of the ledge.

"I don't neither," Taylor said, "but I thought I heard something up there. The scrape of a shoe on the rock or . . . hell, I don't know. It might've been nothing but my imagination."

Hahn's expression was frozen in place. "Jessie and Loozy might be up there, John. I'm going to go look. You stand guard down here, please. Just in case, you know, somebody pops up and tries to shoot me or something."

Taylor nodded and quietly checked the loads in his shotgun. He knew the gun held fresh shells, but he wanted to double-check anyway. He draped his thumb over the twin hammers and said, "Go ahead, then, Dick. I'll keep watch from down here."

"Could I have that pistol, please? There are only five cartridges in the rifle."

"Do you want the gunbelt too?"

"Yes, please."

Taylor unbuckled the belt and handed over the revolver and holster he had taken from the dead robber who tried to kill them in the dead-end canyon, then held the rifle so Hahn would have his hands free to strap the gun belt around his lean hips. The revolver drooped almost to his knees, but the belt would not tighten any farther than he already had it.

Taylor smiled and said, "You look like something on the cover of one of those dime novels."

"I feel silly but I would rather be silly than dead. Just in case. You know."

"Yeah. I know. Go on now." Taylor resumed his hold on the shotgun in his big hands.

Hahn turned and began climbing toward the ledge above.

* * *

Bits of gravel skittered down the mountainside, dislodged by Hahn as he climbed what looked like a nearly vertical path from the trail below to the ledge above. Taylor heard their fall but paid no attention. His eyes were riveted on Dick Hahn's back.

It occurred to him that he did not know how wide the spread of buckshot would be if someone did show himself on the ledge and Taylor be forced to shoot him. Might Hahn be shot too. In the back. And wouldn't that be horribly convenient for a coroner's inquest to consider, Hahn being his rival for Jessica's affections and Taylor being the one who shot the man in the back? He could just imagine how a prosecutor might view that nasty circumstance.

"Be careful, Dick," he called but no louder, he hoped, than would reach Hahn's ears. If one of the kidnappers, the man Ederle, for instance, indeed was up there, Taylor did not want to tip him to their presence below.

Taylor was rapt in thoughts and worries to the point that he was distracted.

His attention was brought fully back by the dull, almost hollow sound of a gunshot.

And Dick Hahn came tumbling back down to land in a heap at John Taylor's feet.

Ervin Ederle

Erv stood, straightened his back, and then stamped his feet a few times to get the circulation moving in his legs. That was something he had noticed in the past year or two. He tended to cramp sometimes and he did not have as much strength in his legs as he used to. That was another good reason why he needed to retire to Mexico.

But whiskey helped. It surely did. He took another small pull on one of the bottles he had brought back from Phil Embry's store. Good. Phil put together trade whiskey that was almost as smooth as the bonded stuff. He took another sip and set the bottle aside. It would not pay to drink too much here. Not when he had so much at stake in those two females. They were the currency his future would be bought with.

He heard voices murmuring. The woman and kid he supposed. Except . . .

He glanced toward the back of the adit where the two were huddled up against the wall covered to the gills with some of the old coal sacks.

They were not talking, he saw. The kid even seemed to be dozing. So who in the hell was doing that talking? Surely he wasn't hearing things.

Frowning, Erv eased out into the sunlight and over toward the lip of the ledge.

He could definitely hear voices now. Male voices. He was sure of it.

He pulled his pistol out of its leather pouch and slowly,

very slowly, inched farther out onto the ledge, out toward where they had pretty much worn a path from all the wood carrying and hauling of the supplies he had brought back from Phil's place.

Jesus! He saw the top of a hat come into view. A black derby hat like the little banker wore. Madre de Dios!

Erv brought up his revolver, thumbed the hammer, and snapped a shot off at the little bastard before he had time to think about it. Or to let more of the banker show above the rim so Erv would have more of a target to shoot at.

The banker disappeared in an instant and Erv heard a frightened yelp. Good. That must have been a hit. Now where was the big fellow so Erv could kill him too?

Chapter 27

Taylor threw the shotgun to his shoulder and pointed it toward the rim of the ledge fifteen or twenty feet above. There was no target there to fire at . . . which was just as well because when he brought the gun down he realized he had forgotten to cock the hammers.

He shuddered and knelt beside Hahn. "Are you okay, Dick? Where were you hit?"

Hahn sat up, rubbed his face, and wiggled his shoulders. "I think I am, actually. All right, I mean. I wasn't hit. God, John, I did hear the bullet go past. It was that close. It sounded like the world's biggest bumblebee. I mean . . . zip . . . and it was gone. Just like that."

"You look awfully pale."

"Did you see the guy who shot at me?"

Taylor shook his head. "No. I just heard the gunshot and saw you tumble down here. Are you sure you aren't hurt?"

"My leg and right hip hurt a little where I fell on them, but nothing is broken. I'm all right. Really. Do you think we can get a look at him? Or a shot, maybe?"

Again Taylor had to shake his head no. "He's up on that ledge where we can't see, much less get a shot at him. And we can't back off far enough to get a look up there. We can go down the mountain but not out to the side here. That's what it would take to get a better angle of view."

"What about the girls? You can't see them?"

"Haven't seen nor heard them. Truth is, we might be

barking up the wrong tree here. That fella up there is a thief. We know that. Hell, he stole your purse the other day. Maybe he thinks we've come after him because of that. Maybe he doesn't have anything to do with the kidnapping."

Hahn tried to stand, winced at the pain on his right side but managed to get upright. He felt a little better once he was standing again. He reached down for the rifle he had dropped when he fell and examined it to make sure it was all right. "So how do we find out?"

Taylor thought about the question for a moment, then took a deep breath and bellowed as loudly as he could, "Jessica! Loozy! Are you there?"

"Papa?" a shrill voice answered quickly, followed by the sound of flesh striking flesh and a cry of sudden pain.

"I guess that answers that," Dick Hahn said, his expression a mixture of determination, fear, and hatred. Determination to end this. Fear of how it might end. Hatred for the man who held his beloved Jessica. "What do we do now?"

"We can't charge up there after them. The guy would just shoot us as we come into his view. That would make it easy for him," Taylor said.

"Give me a minute," Hahn said. "Let me think about this."

Taylor stood holding the shotgun and peering up toward the ledge where Jessica and Louse were being held. He felt more helpless now than he had when he read the note about the kidnapping.

* * *

Dick Hahn moved back from the relatively sheltered spot against the slope of the mountain. He swallowed his nervousness as best he was able, paused for a moment more, then shouted, "You up there. Ederle? We've come to pay the ransom."

There was no immediate response, so he tried again. "We brought your money, Ederle."

The big man's gravelly voice came back, "How much?"

"Everything I could get hold of," Hahn shouted.

"Toss it up here. If I think it's enough I'll send the hostages down."

"We don't trust you. You robbed us once. How do we know you won't cheat us now?"

"You got no damn choice. Not if you want this woman and the kid," Ederle responded.

"Let me think about it," Hahn answered. He stepped close to the mountainside again.

"How much do you have with you?" Taylor asked.

Hahn looked worried when he said, "About four hundred sixty dollars. It is all . . . Jess and I are doing well enough, but we haven't saved so very much. We've mostly spent what I bring in."

"Give me a hundred," Taylor said. "Biggest bills you have. A single hundred if you have it."

Hahn reached inside his trousers and produced a thin sheaf of paper money. He selected a pair of fifties and handed them to John Taylor. Taylor stuffed the bills into his pocket and began running downhill toward their horses.

* * *

"For a minute there I was worried you weren't coming back," Hahn said as Taylor came laboring up the hill, puffing and gasping for breath in the high, thin air.

"Had to . . . get . . . this stuff." Taylor knelt and selected a fist-sized rock from the ground. He took Hahn's money out of one pocket and from another produced a pair of horseshoe nails. From that same pocket he withdrew a greasy piece of cloth that he used to clean tack and other items.

He used the horseshoe nails to pin the two fifty-dollar bills to the cloth, then wrapped the cloth around the rock and tied the opposing ends together. "There," he said with a grunt when he was done. He stepped back again, looking up at the ledge where Ederle was holding Jessica and Loozy.

"You up there, Ederle?" he shouted.

"What do you want?"

"Here. Here's a show of good faith." He tossed the small, heavy bundle onto the ledge.

There was only silence from the kidnapper.

Ervin Ederle

Erv's lips drew back into a wicked grin when he saw the pale cloth come sailing over the rim to land on the ledge. Too close to the edge, though. He was not sure of the angles involved; one of them might be able to see him if he rushed forward to grab the cloth and whatever it contained. That might be what they wanted. Maybe they were trying to get him out there so they could get a clear shot at him. Erv turned his head.

The woman and the girl were huddled close to the mouth of the adit now. They had heard everything that was going on.

"Kid," he growled. "Get out there and get that thing."

"Me?" The kid looked frightened. So did her mother, for that matter.

"Hell yes, you," Erv growled. "Go on now. And don't forget, I got your mama here. Now step out there an' get me that whatever-it-is."

Louise looked at her mother for direction, then reluctantly stood. She walked past the ashes of their fire ring and out onto the ledge where he wanted her to go. She stood looking down—at her father probably or the banker—and for a moment he thought she was going to try to get down there to them.

Erv would have shot the little bitch if she tried to do that. Instead she only bent over, picked up the rock, and brought it back to him.

He accepted the bundle from her and motioned for her to go back to her mother, which she very quickly did.

He untied the knots in the cloth and removed the rock, tossing it aside. He spread the cloth open and smiled when he saw the pair of crisp fifty-dollar goldbacks.

Erv did not know where the little bastard had kept his stash of currency or he could have gotten it that night down at Phil's place. Not that it mattered now. It would be his, all of it, as soon as they agreed to the transfer.

And then . . . then he supposed the sensible thing would be to shoot them all, the men and the females too.

He carefully unpinned the notes from the cloth and tucked them into his pocket, then flipped open the loading gate on his revolver. He needed the weapon to be fully loaded.

Chapter 28

John Taylor almost cried with relief when he saw the top of Loozy's sweet head and even got a glimpse of her face when she came close to the rim of the ledge to pick up the ante in this game.

"Ederle," he called out after a minute or two. "There's plenty more of those fifties. You can have them."

"Send them up. Then I'll send the woman and kid down."

Taylor waited a moment before he spoke again, then said, "Look'a here, Ederle. Say, d'you mind if I ask you something?"

"What's that?"

"What is your first name? Embry told us but I've forgot."

"What's it matter to you?"

"It doesn't matter really but I'd rather call you that if you don't mind. I'm trying to be friendly. What is it?"

"You can call me Erv. It's short for Ervin."

"All right, Erv, thanks. Erv, I think we can work this out so that we both of us get what we want. It's clear enough what that would be. Me and Dick here want Jessica and Louise back. We want you to turn them over to us like you said in that note. How you divide the money up between you and the other guys is up to you. Since they aren't here I suppose you could even take all the money and skeedaddle. Of course that's up t' you. It's only an idea."

Ederle laughed, the sound reaching Taylor and Hahn below. "I fooled you assholes, didn't I? There's no gang. Nobody was watching you. I just said that to keep you in line. I'm not so dumb, see. I had you jumping through my hoops and you didn't even know it."

"That's right, Erv. You did fool us. So all this money will be yours anyway. There isn't anybody you have to split it with."

"How much money are we talking about?" Ederle called.

"A lot, Erv. It's a little over twenty thousand and we have it right here." He looked at Hahn and gave the little man an apologetic shrug. Hahn nodded back, his expression grim.

"More than twenty, you say? How much more?"

"It's actually twenty-one thousand five hundred sixty dollars," Taylor said, pulling the number out of the thin mountain air.

"That's a lot of money. Is it in gold?"

"No, it's all currency. Lighter to carry, you know. And smaller. Easier to hide, which you already found out or you would have taken it the night you got Dick's purse."

"Where is it now?"

"It's in a pair o' saddlebags. What I'm thinking, Erv, is that we can put the saddlebags down in plain sight so we can't snatch them back at the last second. Then you send the girls down, see. We take them but leave the saddlebags. You can keep an eye on them while we take the girls and ride away. Everybody gets what he wants, Erv, and nobody gets hurt. How does that sound to you?"

"Let me think about it," Ederle called down from the ledge.

"It's a good offer, Erv. Lot of money. You can have it all, Erv. More than twenty thousand." He hoped the bastard didn't want to hear the total again because he had forgotten how much he claimed was there.

Taylor stepped over close to the mountainside next to Dick Hahn and whispered, "How'd I do?"

"I didn't know how well you can lie," Hahn whispered back. "You almost convinced me, and I know how much we have here."

"Cross your fingers, Dick, an' hope the son of a bitch goes for it."

* * *

"Here's the deal," Ederle called down to them. "I don't trust you not to shoot me once you have the woman, so I want you to leave your guns where they are. Lay them on the path there. In plain sight, mind. Then you walk away and I send them down to you. You take them, see, and you leave."

"We could do that," Hahn yelled. "Anything you say, Mr. Ederle."

"Mister, is it now?"

"Yes, of course. We'll put the saddlebags wherever you want them. Someplace you can see that we don't grab them back and try to get away. We won't cheat you, Mr. Ederle. All we want is to get Jessica and Loozy back. No tricks. We'll do whatever you want."

"You'll leave your guns behind?"

"Yes, of course."

"I want you to put the saddlebags, um, do you see that white rock with the green stuff growing on it?"

"The lichen, you mean? Yes, I see it."

"One of you put the saddlebags there. Right on top where I can keep an eye on it. There's really twenty-one thousand in those bags?"

"I guarantee it," Hahn replied. "You have my word on it."

Ederle laughed. "What I got is your woman on it. Any tricks and she's dead. You know that, don't you?"

"We know that, Mr. Ederle."

"What about the other one?"

"I understand it too, Erv," Taylor shouted.

"Get the saddlebags, then. Leave your guns where they are. I don't want you going down there armed."

"This will take a few minutes," Taylor said. "I have to go all the way down to the horses."

"Hell, I ain't in no hurry. I've waited up here this long, haven't I? A few more minutes won't matter."

"All right. All right. I'm going." Taylor leaned the shotgun up against the mountain slope. Dick Hahn quickly set the rifle there in its place and picked up the much more familiar shotgun that Taylor had borrowed from him. He felt better with it in his hands.

Hahn looked worried. Taylor gripped the smaller man's shoulder and lightly squeezed. Then he turned away and started down the mountain as quickly as he safely could.

* * *

Taylor emerged from the trees and came huffing and puffing his way back up the mountainside with a pair of bulky saddlebags draped over his left shoulder. His hands were free and he wore no gun belt. That was still sagging around Dick Hahn's narrow waist.

He could see Erv Ederle standing near the rim of the ledge, watching closely to make sure there were no tricks. Ederle held a revolver in his hand.

When he got to the pale boulder Ederle had indicated, Taylor stopped and ostentatiously removed the saddlebags from his shoulder and held them high for Ederle to see. The left side bag held his dirty laundry, the right his spare horseshoe, nails, and rasp in case of the need for hoof repair along the way.

Taylor placed the bags on top of the waist-high boulder, spreading them apart so Ederle could see both halves at once. Then he started back up toward Dick Hahn.

"Stay where you are," Ederle shouted. "Don't come back up. Go back."

Taylor gave Hahn a helpless look. Then he turned around and started back down to the trees.

Jessica Taylor

They were down there. So close. So helpless. She had seen the calculating look on the man's face. Seen the way he so very carefully reloaded that pistol. He intended to use the gun. She was sure of it. He intended to kill Dick. John as well, probably. And if he did that he would surely kill her and Loozy too.

Jessica squeezed her eyes tightly closed and began to cry, neither of which helped in the slightest.

She opened her eyes again and leaned away from the rock wall where she had been sitting. She disengaged herself from the arm Loozy had over her shoulders and came into a crouch.

The man, that son of a bitch kidnapping man, was standing at the edge, looking down at the men. Men who loved her. Men who were going to die because of loving her.

No. It was too much.

Jess patted Loozy's knee.

Then she launched herself at the bastard's back.

Chapter 29

Hahn heard a grunt, an explosion of suddenly expelled air, and something large and dark came flying off the rim overhead.

Long-standing habits of hand and mind, honed on thousands of clay pigeons and club pigeon shoots, took over as if an instinct. The shotgun came easily to his shoulder, his thumbs snapping both hammers back on the way.

He fired. Back trigger first. The gun rocked hard against his shoulder. No pause. Front trigger next. And a bloody form fell virtually at his feet.

Richard Hahn looked down as the figure began to slide downhill.

He gagged and struggled to keep from throwing up.

Taylor came rushing up the slope to him.

Above them Loozy and Jessica stood staring down at the thing that had been their captor.

* * *

Taylor stood clutching Loozy to him as if he would never let go of the child while Dick Hahn and Jessica clung tight to each other.

Taylor looked at the two of them, Jess an inch or so taller than Dick.

She was pretty enough to take a man's breath away. Even after all this, her hair wild as a bird's nest and her face blackened with soot and ash from cooking over a campfire. Even now she was beautiful.

And Dick. One day he would be a rich man. Taylor was sure of it. Someday Dick would be able to provide Jessica, and Loozy too, with all the comforts Jess craved. John never would and they all knew it.

He bent down and kissed Loozy on the forehead, then walked with her to stand in front of Jessica and Dick. He cleared his throat to get their attention, but they were so rapt with each other that he had to do it a second time and even that did not work.

"Mama, Daddy is trying to say something."

Jessica pulled herself away from Dick. "Yes, John?"

"I think . . . damn it, he isn't the total son of a bitch I've thought," he stammered. "And you, well, you have a right to your happiness, I reckon. When we get back down, you go ahead an' have those divorce papers drawn up. I'll sign them."

He kissed his daughter again, turned away, and started down the hill toward the horses.

A lone tear trickled its way down his cheek.

TELL THE WORLD THIS BOOK WAS

GOOD	BAD	SO-SO
		✓

About the Author

Frank Roderus has been writing full time for more than thirty years. Before turning to fiction he received the Colorado Press Association's highest award and as a writer of western novels has twice won the Western Writers of America's Spur Award. He is a member of the WWA and is president of the international professional writing association Western Fictioneers. He is also a life member of the American Quarter Horse Association. He lives in Florida. West Florida, of course.

INTERACT WITH DORCHESTER ONLINE!

Want to learn more about your favorite
books and authors?
Want to talk with other readers that like
to read the same books as you?
Want to see up-to-the-minute Dorchester
news?

VISIT DORCHESTER AT:
DorchesterPub.com
Twitter.com/DorchesterPub
Facebook.com (Search Pages)

DISCUSS DORCHESTER'S NOVELS AT:
Dorchester Forums at DorchesterPub.com
GoodReads.com
LibraryThing.com
Myspace.com/books
Shelfari.com
WeRead.com

CPSIA information can be obtained at www.ICGtesting.com
Printed in the USA
BVOW041500250911

272029BV00003B/1/P

9 781428 511798